# The Seven Saviors

*By*

*Regin Kovacs*

**Published in the United States of America**

ISBN 979-8-9936818-0-1 (SC)

ISBN 979-8-9936818-1-8 (HC)

ISBN 979-8-9936818-2-5 (Ebook)

For Book Rights Adaption and other Rights Permission.

Call us at toll-free **601-914-6178**.

# *Dedicated*

to my daughter, Beverly, without whom this book would never have been written, and for being my first reader

Thank you, *my beloved*.

The locations in this book all exist as real places. The events surrounding these locations are the imagination of the author. While this text is based upon activities during World War II, the actual activities surrounding those events are the imagination of the author.

# Table of Contents

# Prologue

The young girl ran as quickly as the ground would permit her with all its various fallen branches, potholes, rotting log pieces, and other detritus that litters a forest floor.

She was running for the only safety she knew, her secret hut. She had a head-start on the woman chasing her, and she knew the woman would not follow her too far into the woods due to her superstitious nature. But she might just come far enough to grab the girl's hood on the back of her coat, and the girl couldn't risk that. For, if caught, the girl knew what would happen, and it would hurt so bad.

Thus, she kept running until she arrived far into the forest enough where she knew the woman would turn back. Her mother had never gotten past the "house rim," as the girl called the broad log that anyone would have to step high over to pass closer to her "house". So, the girl turned and ducked behind a large, fallen branch to see if her mother would defy her own limits and venture where she had not gone before. *Nope!* The girl was right, as usual, her mother looked, strained her body to see over the brush and pine-laden forest floor, but not succeeding, turned around vanquished and strode back with a grim purposeful demeanor.

The young girl tried not to think of the consequences to come, but entered her "house" with a smile as she left the real world behind, and entered the reverie continuing in her imaginary "house".

# Chapter I

Cully tried to cry, but nothing would come. She felt it was "her duty" to cry as it was her mother who died. She disliked the phrase "passed"; therefore, she simply refused to ever use it. Her mother went quickly, at least. She had a cerebral aneurysm burst while changing the bathroom light bulb. The pathologist's report stated that her mother was more than likely dead before she hit the floor. Her father had died from lung cancer some twenty years ago to the month of her mother's demise. She thought that coincidences like that were odd and possibly a symbol of some spiritual nature, but she could not defend that thought with any biblical evidence. She just thought it. Like the time her adopted Jewish cousin, who Cully could not tolerate to be in the presence of, visited Cully's parents when he was a young man. The cousin talked about how well off he would be when his own parents, an elderly couple, passed away. He talked of selling their house, and reaping the heavy insurance his father put on his personal belongings, which would net him a tidy benefit. *How ironic*, Cully thought, with a sad little smirk, *that my cousin was diagnosed with leukemia within two years and died at Sloan-Kettering Cancer Center in New York. My cousin's parents were alive and well, both 89.* She thought it sad for them to lose their son, but believed they really did not know their son as well as she did from their youth. She knew that her cousin was clever enough to feign a compassionate nature, but, in essence, was a pathological liar. There it was, spiritual significance of turn-about Cully could not deny to herself.

2

It had been two years ago now, and Cully still wanted to grieve for her mother, but she felt that pang of anger rise up again. She lost her actual mother years before, soon after her dad died. Her mother made a brave face of it for a few years, but then it was all too much for her mother when men started paying attention to her. They would ask her out on dates in her senior living community. Her mother rejected all such advances. Cully thought it was because her mother never knew another man, having been with her father since she was just fifteen-years-old. Her parents married in 1962. Since then, they had been inseparable.

In the years after they lost their father to cancer, Cully's older sister, Sybil, was visiting. In chatting, Sybil mentioned a past event concerning their mother, Adele, when Cully was a teenager. The two of them discovered that their multiple conversations, independently with their mom, did not match the information that each had received over past years. They determined that their mother must have needed to feel indispensable to all of them, so she had manipulated and betrayed all her children by misrepresenting information about one sibling to another, thereby discouraging contact between the children themselves. Her mother succeeded in her devious interference; her deceptive acts kept any close relationship among the adult children from developing. She took the position of being the conduit among her children. Thus, Cully and Sybil ascertained through their most recent exchange, that their mother wanted desperately to remain the center of attention in her children's lives to bolster her self-importance by exercising whatever means to keep that central position. She had been making herself essential to all family communication.

Mom's act had been polished though. To everyone else around her, who weren't family, her mother was seen as a dedicated, brilliant "social butterfly," senior citizen with four attentive children.

After Sybil informed their two brothers, Jack and Fox, of girls' mind-boggling revelattion, the men's feelings about their mother's antics sat hard. The men's tears welled-up, anger followed, and feelings of betrayal grew, taking deep root and fostering complete distrust of their mother. *Who would imagine one's own mother would lie to their children for years to keep siblings apart?!* From that point forward, Cully, Sybil, Jack, and Fox had agreed to keep their mother "out-of-the-loop" permanently. The fact that they could not approach their mother anymore regarding another sibling was heart wrenching. Finally, acceptance descended on them all that mom, for all her bravado and persistent claims that she was like a martyr, revealed that, in fact, she was a deeply needy person. As the siblings initiated this exclusion of their mother from sibling communication, she became dramatically critical of her children, made rude comments, and asserted that her opinion on an issue was actual fact. She became emotionally unstable and verbally abusive to her children in reaction to their individual control of communication with each other. Her behavior only became more bizarre and uglier as she aged.

Upon their mother's death from a cerebral aneurysm, that occurred while she was changing a light bulb in the bathroom, it became apparent to all of Cully's siblings that the family relationship damage their mother caused had become beyond repair. Cully and the others were too advanced into adulthood to recover a deep familial closeness. This made it all the more challenging because of the geographical distances among them. The brothers lived on the west coast miles apart and the sisters lived in the Midwest and Texas.

There was no memorial nor funeral staged for their mother by Cully and her siblings. Other than the overwhelming legal issues she left them, the death was noted only by a favorite aunt and uncle and their grown children on their father's side. These were additional people their mother had ostracized, as she aged as a widow. Thus, the siblings remained cordial acquaintances, but Cully gave up trying to reassert a closeness she only experienced as a child to the family that remained.

And now, she was a thirty-nine-year-old widow herself, going on a month. Her husband, Richard, died suddenly from a heart attack while drinking a cup of coffee at work. They had produced two children, one named Mina, at Cully's mother's suggestion, one little boy named Byron, who lived for an hour and a half due to his premature delivery, and an adopted little boy they named David. They gave both their children love through logical boundaries, and had decided early in their marriage not to interfere in the sibling's relationship after the challenge of their teen years. Although, Cully and Richard were always there for them, they let them know, unabashedly, what they needed from their kids as adults: hugs, phone calls, and to be an active part of their lives. The couples' proudest achievement was giving their adult children the freedom of communication with each other, freedom to explore whoever they wanted to be without judgment on their choices. If Cully or Richard wanted to give them guidance, they achieved it through questioning and soliciting answers about their various decisions. They taught them decision-making skills, that developed the children's ability to contemplate the merit of their own choices. So, with drive, ambition, and self-confidence, Mina and David grew up and, ironically, both moved to California for career opportunities.

Upon the children's funereal visit for their much-loved father, Cully hugged them at least a dozen times. She was devasted. On what turned out to be a glorious day it did not give any consolation. It seemed wrong to Cully. She wanted the world to mourn her husband's death. She wanted people to stop working and give a moment of silence for her wonderful husband had died. She had that same exact feeling when their son, Byron, did not survive but an hour and a half after birth. As unrealistic as her wishes were, she had wanted it to at least rain, so the weather matched her tears, so that it would feel like everyone present was mourning her beautiful husband.

5

Subsequently, Cully sent Mina and David back to their lives in California where they engrossed themselves in administrative jobs in the film industry. They had grown up together as best friends. Both graduated from Niles West High School, then from Northern Illinois University. Both had ambitious desires. That was all right with Cully. She refused to burden her children with a feeling of having to change their lives to accommodate her sadness and any loneliness or fear she might experience in this new phase of her life. Despite her semi-annual visits to California, her children could only make periodic holiday returns.

Three weeks after Richard's, funeral, Cully sat on their bed, *her bed now*, reached for a tissue for the hundredth time, stared at it, laughed a little, and spoke to it, "Today is not your day to be used." She threw it back on the side-table, and continued packing up her deceased husband's possessions for the give-away.

# *Chapter II*

Bang! The door hit Cully in the butt, and she yelled, "OW!"

"OW!" escaped from her lips again, as she stayed motionless in the doorway. She did not budge from between the door and the opening.

"I am so sorry!" a man said. "If I had known it was going to close that hard, I would never have let it go." He pulled the door open, and waited for Cully to move, but he did not rush her.

She straightened her back, and looked at him with a blank face, not wanting to judge before she read exactly what was in his face, old, young, arrogant, shocked, remorseful, or careless. His face was a mix of many things, but fear covered his face the most.

"It's going to take a minute for me to move," she smiled weakly. The door hit me in a tender area of my backside."

The man looked down. The dawning of his understanding crept up his face in a sheepish smile. He nodded to Cully, patiently. Customers, who wanted to leave the coffee shop, saw her face and just decided to wait until she was ready to move. Cully finally moved out of the way but very slowly, and as she did, she heard some of the customers snickering about her predicament. Cully raised her head and walked past them as if nothing had happened. The man just stood there, his eyes following her back like she forgot to yell at him. He turned and went to the queue for his coffee, turning once to take a peek at her. All he saw was that she took a seat, carefully, in the very back of the café. She put her head in her hands to get her bearing, and winced a little at the back pain. She noticed that a few customers were staring at her. She ignored them as she removed her scarf and gloves to lie on the table. As she was called, she rose slowly to join the pick-up queue for her afternoon indulgence before her train.

Once Cully went back to her booth, which was still empty, her scarf and gloves were exactly where she laid them. She sat down with her coffee and pastry too quickly. She tried to keep quiet as she, "a-h-h-hed" and "o-o-o-o-oed," while repositioning her backside carefully. She always became aggravated that despite her backside being slightly generous in size, it did not protect her from pain! Not during a good massage, not from a rough seat, not even from bumping into the corner of her own couch at home. *Oh well, she thought, this too shall pass*. This was a statement that she would often repeat which her father passed on to her as a child when she was angry or sad. It helped her face life's little ups and downs.

Cully did not have a contemporary, skinny-jean physique. She had curves like an hourglass. Her husband, Richard, frequently told her she looked more like a woman from the 50s or early 60s, like Gina Lollobrigida, and he liked those curves very much.

Cully, settled into her booth and stared out the window. She wondered where her life was going now. She had no new direction. She didn't know if she even needed a new direction. She had a well-paying job, which gave her the security of being able to keep her house payments up. Along with Richard's life insurance, which would provide for her other expenses, there would be no interruption in her comfortable living. She figured she was just typical middle class. Her job was "ok". She worked as an executive assistant to a Chief Financial Officer at a bank. She enjoyed responsibility. Her job was in downtown Chicago, and she loved that. She had windows to lookout over the city, plush taupe carpeting, even the cubicles on the floor made her feel like she was part of some upper echelon. And classy. Everyone she worked with looked like they were going out for cocktails at an up-scale restaurant. She tried to dress that way, so she scoured the internet for discounts on the clothes she bought. She was secretly proud that she never paid full retail price for things other women bragged about purchasing at exorbitant prices. *How dumb*, she thought. She'd rather have the money than pay designer prices. But her feelings took on a dramatic change since her husband's death. She felt maudlin and thought her job was pointless and empty, considering she had no one locally left in her life. Her husband and children had been her life. Her work friends' condolences only made her avoid them.

Cully gazed at the corner through the smudges on the cafe window. People were rushing to cross Adams Street, the yellow cabs whizzing by, the ornate, historical structure of some of the buildings mixed in with the new chrome and glass ones, all contributed to that feeling of moving, going somewhere, being somebody. She was a part of this metropolis, she thought, and she normally used to love every minute of it. Especially in the spring. It was her favorite time downtown, not too hot, not too cold, just pleasant.

Now she was a widow at a young age. There was no more cozy feeling of leaving the city behind and arriving home in Skokie her husband. At a time like that, she would be swept up in his arms with a glass of white German wine waiting for her before they ate dinner. She had someone to go home to. She had someone who worried where she was. She had someone who called her during the day for no particular reason than to just hear her voice. A shiver ran down her spine. Okay, she was a little frightened of the severe change in her life. As much as she tried to prevent them, she started to get a panic attack. The more she contemplated her new life without Richard, tears flooded her eyes, yet she had a need to get a grip on herself. She ate her pastry, and drank her coffee slowly to gain control. However, Cully relented and took one of her emergency anxiety pills she carried with her. Her panic attacks, which came infrequently, always started in her stomach and slowly spread out from there, so if she took the pill soon enough, it quelled her stomach within minutes, which led the nervous tentacles to withdraw. She waited a few minutes. She could feel her stomach calming down. *Thank God for modern medicine, she thought.* Taking a deep breath, Cully noticed it was getting late, and her afternoon snack time was over. She had to get to Union Station to get her train home, where her three-bedroom, two-bath bungalow served as her sanctuary, where she could also retrieve that last glass of wine from the fridge.

She quickly picked up her leavings, disposed of them in the trash and did a short reconnaissance before walking out the door. The man who let the door slam on her was still at his table. He too had been gazing out the window, but once she got near the door, he turned and gave her a small smile. She sort-of smiled in return, thought how attractive he was, and turned to open the door to leave. She realized that she had stayed for her "before going home" snack too long, and she had to power walk-almost run-all the way to the station. Doing so, she wondered how old her door-attacker was, if he was happily married, if he was gay and happily married. Lucky him, she thought; she just assumed he was one or the other.

By the time she reached her train car, she was out of breath and her calves hurt her to the point that she had to massage them at her seat. Fortunately, she was able to sit alone, and once again, began to wonder whether she should do something else with her life while she was massaging her left calf. She didn't want to add something extra that would tax her current life. She needed a complete change if she was going to do anything. Maybe, it would help her heal faster if she left the world of work she was so used to and sold the house, bought a different house, somewhere other than Skokie. Although, moving to California just to be near the kids, was not her idea of a life for her. As much as she loved her children, she was not interested in crowded interstates, mudslides, deserts, and one season year 'round. As she rested her elbow on the train windowsill with an exasperated sigh, she contemplated all of this. Her head filled with a myriad of ideas to brainstorm, even illogical ones. She remembered, from reading her favorite historical biographies, that Ben Franklin had said at the congressional gathering to declare independence from England, *one must consider and throw out the bad ideas to get to the good ideas.* She laughed to herself as she imagined a job catching elephant poop for nutritionists at a zoo to examine. Her laugh died down; she shook her head and realized how tired she was. She decided the sooner she got home, she would switch that glass of wine out for a nice cold bottle of beer. Imagine that, she thought to herself, a lady of class. She cut out drinking cheap beer, as she became seasoned, satisfied with a glass of wine, including sherry, or a freezing bottle of Heineken beer! Cully's friends would tease her occasionally for not drinking the champagne or fancy martinis at parties, but she didn't care about 'going along with the crowd' anymore. What she had gone through losing her husband after too few years made her lose any uncomfortable feeling of being different, or speaking her mind to people with a higher status than she in the company. She decided fear was a liar, and, if she was afraid of something, she would do it, or face it and be unapologetic toward anyone. She figured that if she could survive missing her husband, nothing else could even come close to making her feel like she wanted to crouch in a corner chair like a frightened child. She was forming a feeling in her mind of determination to look for opportunities to prove she was a survivor.

Cully's eyes glanced over to a reflection in her window of an elderly couple staring at her from across the aisle and down at the end of the seating. She turned her head gradually, but they appeared to be engaged in a conversation with each other. She felt a little odd because of what she thought she saw. She turned her head back to her reflection in the window, and there they were again staring at her! She flicked her head quickly hoping to catch them, but the strangest look covered her face. They were still focused on one another. Cully was wrong about being completely fearless; the apparent discrepancies in the window's reflection and what she saw with her eyes unnerved her a bit. She visited the reflection again, but it was gone as was the couple when she snapped her head back forward. She thought she just imagined it, but she saw it! She was sure they were staring at her. Well, she was too tired to think about it any longer, shook it off, and rose to exit the train as the conductor called out her station.

# Chapter III

As soon as Cully got home, she dragged herself upstairs to close the curtains of her dormer windows. She happened to gaze out at the orangish sky, and became startled. She saw the same elderly couple standing kitty-corner from her house. She couldn't believe her eyes! She closed her eyes and opened them once again. The couple had vanished. She thought she was going crazy, or just imagining it, since she was so tired, but no! Stumbling back from the window, she was sure she saw what she saw.

She grabbed her Heineken and began drinking it quickly for something to do. She thought. She made a decision. She would wait one more day, and, if it happened again, she would call the police. *But wait, she thought,* put in a complaint about an elderly couple staring at her? They'd probably laugh at her. Hell, she would laugh at her. She quickly ran down the stairs, grabbed another beer from the fridge, locked the doors, and scrambled back up to her bedroom. *Awwww, that beer was good,* she thought as she drained it, lay her head down, and promptly fell asleep.

Next morning, running late, Cully changed her clothes to fresh ones, grabbed her purse, flew down the hall for her coffee holder, and stopped abruptly looking out the front window. There was the old couple again, standing across the street! She left her jacket and mug, and opened her door, walked swiftly across the heavily treed residential street and confronted the gray-haired couple.

"Excuse me," she said, not too gently and slightly out of breath, "But, I feel like you've been following me since yesterday, and, I saw you here last night. What do you want with me? If you need help, or need to tell me something, or ask for something, speak up!"

The elderly couple looked at her surprisingly, then a little sorrowfully, then at each other, and back to her. The well-dressed gentleman spoke with a thick German accent, "I am sorry. We didn't want to scare you. We just wanted to find out if you were who we thought you were."

"And, who, pray tell, is that?"

"Are you Clotilda Schellenburg?"

"Who? Oh, no, well, actually it's Cully. I have never used the name, Clotilda. I have no idea why my mother ever named me that. My parent's name is Sherman, but my married name is Rollins now." She touched her chin looking up, "I don't recall if I ever knew my mother's maiden name."

"Have you ever heard of a Mina Beck?" the woman asked with a hard accent.

"No, do you think she is a relative because I don't think so. There's probably a lot of Becks around. My mother definitely never mentioned a Mina Beck. My mother's name was Adele Sherman, then Mars when she married. But she passed away recently, so we can't really ask her," Cully expelled in an angry and nervous rush. *She was going to miss her train.*

Both elderly people looked sympathetic, "We are sorry for you losing your mother. We need to keep looking then. Thank you for approaching us."

"First of all, you could have just come to my door to ask me. Secondly, my mother refused to talk about any relatives in Europe. I have no idea who this Mina Beck is. My mother immigrated to America as a young woman, she told me, and nothing more. So, no, I have never heard of a Mina Beck, my mother never mentioned a Mina Beck to me ever, nor did anyone else."

14

Cully huffed out. She did not want to divulge to them that it was her mother who provided the name for Cully's oldest daughter, Mina.

The old woman looked sadly at the old man. They both looked like they had come off Ellis Island, but this was the 21st century. *Ellis Island had been a museum or something,* Cully thought as she studied them. Their clothes were not torn or tattered, they just looked a lot out of style. The woman had on a white blouse she could see at the collar of her coat, as did the man above his collar of his coat, impeccably clean, unwrinkled, and with a tie. Whether the tie was out of style or not, she couldn't tell, since the flap of his coat covered most of it. The one thing Cully noted most obviously was the lack of lint, dirt, wear and tear, or anything that would make the coat look profoundly used or old.

Nonetheless, she felt they were harmless enough, so she asked, "Can you tell me how you know this, Mina Beck? Maybe, I can point you to city records or something." She felt foolish now, having approached them with anger.

"No, that's OK, "said the sad woman, also with a heavy accent. "We just need to find someone that knows her or a relative of hers."

"Well, I'm sorry I can't help you, really." Cully turned away, then twisted back toward the couple, "By the way, did you happen to be on the CTA train out of Chicago last night? You look just like a couple I saw on my ride home last night. They were staring at me too, I think, I don't really know because every time I looked at them, they were talking to each other; it was strange."

Again, the couple looked at each other, silently, then the woman replied, "Could not have been us. We were not there."

"Perhaps, you were tired and imagining it, mein Leibster," said the man.

"Maybe," Cully said taking note of the foreign word. She dipped her head down and shook it like she was trying to remember something. Instead,

15

she gave them a steady gaze, and hurriedly asked, "Oh, well, do you need a ride somewhere? I was just driving to the station myself, but I could drop you, if it's local," Cully looked at them expectantly.

The old man sighed and said in the same heavy accent, "No thank you. We'll see ourselves where we need to go. But you are very kind." The man gave a small smile to her and turned his head away as did the woman. They shuffled down the side-walk, as Cully crossed back to her side of the street, glancing back, briefly, to see the woman hold up her hand to wave at Cully. Cully waved politely back with a forced smile, then turned. But she stopped suddenly at her front door stoop. She distinctly heard the woman say from afar, "Good-bye, Clotilda. We'll see you again." Cully whipped around so quickly that she threw herself off balance, and had to catch the side of the light post with her hand. The look of her stare accompanied her gaping mouth as she faced the empty sidewalk across the street.

She knew she heard the woman call her by her birth name, Clotilda. Yet, she had legally changed her first name to Cully, after her mother passed, even though she'd been using the name most of her life. Also, she had asked her mother a few times why she named her, Clotilda, but her mother always shrugged and told her she got it from a distant relation, nobody Cully knew. Then her mother would impatiently wave her out of the kitchen and give her a chore to do.

While this story may have been true, the only other people who knew her birth name were Sybil, Jack and Fox. Besides which, the boys were both oceanographers and always away on some water discovering things and writing reports. They only kept in touch with annual birthday cards signed both John (Jack) and Foxworth (Fox). She received no phone calls, nor texts, although, she liked keeping up those yearly birthday cards. She didn't want to totally lose touch with them. All of her siblings lived in different worlds. Furthermore, she was not close to her high-maintenance sister anymore. After their mother's funeral, Sybil and she had a sizable falling out over their already shrinking relationship that was unlikely to be resurrected.

In fact, by the time she was eight, Cully had forgotten that her parents ever named her 'Clotilda' as a newborn. *She had heard, "Cully put that down, or, Cully, time for bed, and, Cully, your eyes will stay like that if you don't uncross them."* When she started kindergarten, however, she did not want to be laughed at as she was sure she would be with a name like 'Clotilda'. So, she begged her mom to write down "Cully" on all her paperwork for school. Therefore, the name 'Clotilda' stayed in her baby book. It had even slipped her mind until a moment ago.

*Not only that, how could the couple know they were not on 'her train'?* She didn't tell them which train she took. Cully stood there watching the sidewalk as if it was going to produce the couple again any minute. But, it didn't. She turned and went back in the house to get her things for work. Now she would have to take the later train. However, a slight apprehension crawled into her feelings.

# Chapter IV

While Cully was reading her messages at her desk that morning, she decided to call the police after all. She would frame it as an inquiry of concern in case the couple might have dementia, Alzheimer's, or were confused about where their grown children lived. She tried to think of reasons for calling other than that. The fact that they knew her birth name, and they were following her was little unsettling. She didn't want to be laughed at or not taken seriously, so she looked up the non-emergency number for the Skokie police, Chicago police? She chose Skokie first.

She dialed the number on her cell phone, and a youngish guy answered the phone, "Skokie Police Department. This is Officer Hastings."

There was a pause. "Hello. Is someone there? I don'……"

"Yes, yes, I'm sorry, this is Cully Rollins. I need to talk to someone about an elderly couple in my neighborhood. I think something is off about them, and they may need help," Cully breathed out.

"Okay, that would be Officer Pullman on today's roster. What's your address? He can come out to talk to you today, I think, let me look, yep. He can be at your house in about 20 minutes. Would that be alright?" the officer said in a monotone.

"No, no. I'm at work right now. Could someone come by tonight around 6:30?"

"I'll have to check. What's your number? I'll have someone call you back."

Cully paused, "Okay, that would be great." She gave him her cell number and hung up, nervous now about making a big deal out of the situation. It was just too weird that the old woman knew her birth name. She had to keep thinking that every time she wanted to call back and cancel the reporting.

A few hours later, while she was trying to chow down on her salad for lunch and sort some data for her boss, the phone rang. Still chewing, she picked it.

"Cully Rollins here."

"Yes, this is Officer Maitland. I was told you had a concern about an elderly couple in your neighborhood."

"Yes, that's correct. I spoke with them on the sidewalk this morning, and they were looking for a specific person or relative. I couldn't help them, but I got the strangest feeling that they were lost, or forgetful and just wandering. I'm just concerned because I saw them last night on that sidewalk and this morning, I spoke to them."

"Okay, Ms. Rollins, why don't I come to your home at about 6:30 tonight to take the details. Would that work for you?"

"Yes, that would be great. Thank you so much." Cully gave them her address. The officer spoke once more, "Thank you, Ms. Rollins, for looking out for the elderly. That's something not everybody would do."

"Well, I just saw a very concerned look in their eyes, and it's bothered me all morning." She couldn't shrug off the feeling that the officer might be dismissive on the other end.

"Okay, I will be out there sometime around 6:30. Thank you, Ms. Rollins," he said with a sigh.

19

"Bye," Cully said and pushed the off button. "Okay, am I really going to do this?" she said out loud to no one in particular. *He probably thinks I'm an idiot, and this is a waste of his time* she thought. Cully began biting at her nails, something she hadn't done in years.

At 6:30 that night, Cully fluffed up her couch pillows, picked up her three pairs of shoes she left in front of the ottoman, threw them into the bedroom down the hall, and generally scanned the front room if it was presentable to receive a guest. It was dark out at this hour, so she put on the porch light and waited on the edge of the couch, picking at her nails again. Not long after, the doorbell rang, and Cully patted her hair in the hall mirror, then answered the door. Officer Daniel Maitland was a bit on the slender and of an indeterminate age neither young nor old. He was patient while she just stared at him. Finally, feeling stupid, she quietly said,

"Oh, hello, Officer. Thank you for coming."

He paused looking at her from an angle, "No problem, Ms. Rollins. Are you okay?"

Cully stood there as if in a trance.

"May I come in?" he said with arched eyebrows.

"Oh, I'm sorry, of course," she said a little anxiously, "I feel this is such a minor ordeal for you to come out, but I didn't know what else to do."

"Perfectly alright. It doesn't seem like it should take more than a few minutes? Am I right?" he smiled at her.

"No, no, I'm sure it won't. Please come in and have a seat."

Officer Maitland surveyed the living room briefly noting the nice furnishings, imitation sculptures of historical figures, earth tone colors, then took his place on the edge of a blue-striped couch.

"Now, Ms. Rollins, can you give me a description of this couple and each time you saw them?"

Cully hesitated, and then began explaining about the train ride, leaving out the part about them staring at her in the train window, then the evening before incident, and talking to them that morning. She continued to describe what they looked like and her best guesstimate of their age. She purposely left out that the woman used her birth name. However, she did give the officer the name of who they were looking for.

"Well, Ms. Rollins," the officer said most politely, "I'll alert social services to send someone around the neighborhood within a couple of streets here, and I'll knock on some doors for a little while. I don't want to alarm anyone with my uniform. Social services might be able to send an intern around house to house. I will definitely have this done tomorrow, and let you know if I find anyone who knows about this couple," he said haltingly. He was walking toward the door when he abruptly turned to face her almost crashing into her, she was following him so close. He apologized, and then said, "It's a little odd to have a couple walking around lost, especially in the clothes you described, but it's possible, since I've seen all kinds of things. Thanks for your time. Oh, also, I'll see if one of the desk officers can make some calls to local living centers and such." He paused in thought, and then he said again, "Although, it is a little odd to have a couple wandering around lost."

Cully, wiping her sweating hands on her pants, shook hands with the slender officer, "Thank you so much, Officer Maitland, I would appreciate it if you would let me know if you find out anything." Walking him to the door, Cully didn't realize she was shaking hands with the officer again before she closed the door. *Why did she feel like such a dope?* Well, she did and she didn't. She was afraid to admit she felt almost like she was in the beginning of a Preston and Child novel. So, a certain chill shook her, and she decided to take a hot shower, and read until she fell asleep.

# *Chapter V*

A sound-*tap, tap, tap,* pulled her from sleep? Cully's head slowly rose off the pillow to listen, hearing only quiet, she plopped her head back down.

*Tap- tap- tap.* There it was again, she thought as her eyes popped open with uneasiness. She threw her robe on, looked at the clock, noting it was just after midnight. *The witching hour,* she thought, then dismissed the phrase with an *Oh, my God* thought.

Slowly, she quietly crept downstairs, clutching her robe. When she neared the solid front door, she stealthily reached her right eye up to the door's viewer hole. She was anxious as she snuck a look, and immediately backed away. *Tap-tap-tap*, she heard, but much softer like the person or persons knew she was right on the other side of the door. So, instead of looking, she spoke, "Who's there?" Silence. She strained a little louder, "Who's there?!" She realized she was almost shouting. She took a deep breath, decided to unlock the front door and fling it open, boldly, taking a few steps out onto the large porch in hopes of startling anyone there.

There was no one there. Cully found herself shouting in a whisper, "What is going on?" she asked the night air. Her eyes roved over the dark landscape, seeing nothing that moved. She calmed down, said to the air, "I don't know what game you are playing, but I'm not participating! You hear me," she emphasized with a whispery quietness. She scanned the area one last time, circled the porch to go back to the door, and was startled because the old couple were standing on her porch. The world tilted, and everything went black as she crumpled onto the wet grass.

Cully felt a cold cloth on her head before she opened her eyes. It felt good, but her eyelids felt heavy. She felt she was caught in a dream at night, and she wanted desperately to wake up. She, finally, popped her eyes open to the welcome sight of her living room. She could feel the side of her couch with her left hand and felt comforted. She gave herself a few minutes to adjust to being awake, relaxed on the couch pillow. Finally, she decided to get up. She was a little confused. She couldn't remember why she was on the couch, until upon sitting up she saw in her peripheral vision somebody at her dining room table. To her astonishment, the old couple were sitting there drinking from what looked like her tea set. Cully leaned back against the couch in a bodily surrender to what she saw.

"So, you're really here. Am I right?" she asked the couple.

"Oh, yes, we are here for you," the old man replied

"Then tell me," she insisted, "Why are you here?"

"We very much need your help, Clotilda," replied the old woman.

"Nobody has called me that since I was a small child. How do you know my birth name, and please call me Cully?"

"Clotilda Kappel is my name. I was led to believe you were named after me," the woman said questioningly.

"Who named me after you? Cully asked insistently.

"Well, your mother, of course. It was a familial name," the woman said.

"What family?" Cully pressed.

Clotilda Kappel looked at the old man shocked and asked him, "Are we too late? Is it impossible?"

The old man said, "No, no, Clotilda, it is not too late. Apparently, Adele refused to tell the girl anything about before she came to America. I think we have time. It just requires a little more preparation in a very little time."

"Oh, I suppose you are right, but we have so much to tell her, and remember, she might be hard to convince now," Clotilda said softly.

"Ah, people, I'm right here. You seem to be talking about me, but not to me. Can I get in on this conversation?" Cully asked as she moved to the table and took a chair, sitting her backside down gently.

The woman quickly got her a cup and saucer, pouring her some tea, setting it in front of her. The woman, looked at Cully and addressed her, "Alright, Cull-y," over which the woman's accent stumbled. "Cully, sorry. Drink your tea, dear. We will explain why we desperately need your help. It will seem like a strange request, you probably will not believe us, at first…"

"Or, at second, third, fourth……," interrupted the old man. "I should introduce myself. I am Hans Obermardt. You may just call me Hans. This is Clotilda Kappel," he said sincerely.

"Okay, you, obviously, are from Europe by your accents. Now, I am really confused. I have never been to Europe; my mother came from Germany, but met my father when she got to the U.S. She did not look back or talk about any relatives, despite my asking her so often she would get angry if I brought it up. My father had a sister, but he said both his parents were killed in a railway accident when he was 17. So, I have an uncle, aunt, and a few cousins, but I do not know them. My father was not close to his sister." Cully said starring at the couple, slowly swinging her head from side to side.

Hans looked at Cully until she stopped and focused on his face.

"You, young lady, were born in Berlin."

"What!" Cully raised her voice. "No… my mother showed me my birth certificate. I was born here in Chicago at Grant Hospital. I saw the certificate!"

"I'm afraid she must have had a fake birth certificate made. Your mother married an American businessman named, John Sherman when she was fifteen. She had gone to the states, sorry, America. She passed for eighteen. She went back to Berlin only one time to see about relatives when she was pregnant with you. She wasn't supposed to fly. So, when she got there, she went into labor and you were born three months early in West Berlin in 1981.

"Are you saying my mother lied to me all these years?" Cully asked, her mouth open in disbelief.

Hans answered, "Your mother wanted to check on her relatives in Berlin. Your birth changed everything. She was told that any family she had was on the East side of the wall. It was too dangerous and there was no way for her to enter the zone. She went crazy and decided to get as far away as possible from Germany and to never return. The stories she experienced as a child and later as a young woman terrified her. She disavowed her past and returned with you to America."

"Wait a minute," Cully interrupted. "I need to process all this. How do you know all this?"

"Because, Liebchen, sweet child, we were born in Germany."

"You were in Europe during World War II?"

"Yes, is it so hard to believe? We are very old but glad to be alive to carry out our goal."

"And, what is your goal, as you say?" Cully asked with a hint of skepticism.

"Well," Hans said, but hesitated, "I don't know if you are ready to hear this, but it must come up soon. We came back here tonight because you called the authorities, and we cannot be near them. They would not understand what we need to do."

"Pray tell, what do you need to do?" Cully asked impatiently.

"We need to save two young girls," Clotilda stated succinctly.

"Excuse me?" Cully questioned.

"We need to save two very brave girls, Cully. They are not safe. We know where they are, but we cannot save them without your help," Hans pleaded.

The two visitors were still wearing their coats despite the warmth of the house. The old man had not even removed his hat. Cully shook her head a little like she was trying to wrap her brain around this information and process it into a realistic situation.

"How do I save two little girls?" Cully asked with a look of confusion on her face.

Hans gazed at Clotilda, then they both looked at Cully. Hans answered, "By going back to Germany with us."

Cully face scrunched in confusion. "How do you even know I'm the one who needs to help you?"

"Because Mina told us," Clotilda stated simply.

"Who told you? I'm sorry, I don't understand any of this. What can I do to save them? Do they need rescuing? Are they being held against their will? I'm afraid I don't understand what I can do. Let alone, I don't even know them."

Hans ignored her first question and said, "It is imperative you come with us to save them, or we cannot save her, you understand?" Hans demanded by pounding his small fist on the table.

"Calm down, Hans." Clotilda patted his arm.

"Okay," Cully asked gently, "Are you sure I am the one? Do you have any proof of their being held? Is it this Mina Beck? And, what do you mean, 'her'?" Cully inquired.

"Yes, we have proof. Well, we think we do," said Clotilda.

"You think you do. Okay, what kind of proof?"

"You would have to have a lot of faith in us. We know of your mother's birth in Berlin. We traced her to here when we found the death notice in the newspaper for Adele Sherman. The newspaper had a picture of her much younger."

"I know, my sister gave that to them. My mother did not like having her picture taken. She took all the pictures of us while we were growing up," Cully sighed. "So, bottom line, I have to fly to Germany with you to help rescue two little girls I never met, who may or may not be being held against their will. Is that about the gist of it?"

"I don't know this 'gist' thing…" Hans started.

"It means the basic goal you have that I need to help you with."

"Oh, okay. No, there will be no flying," Hans said matter-of-factly.

"A ship would take too long, besides which there's my job to consider."

"No, we do not go by ship neither. We go by door," Hans said quietly.

Cully looked at him as if she misunderstood, "I'm sorry, by what?"

Clotilda looked at Cully stoically, and said, "By door."

Cully shook her head and felt as if she was not in the real world. She got up, went to the front window, looked outside, saw a few people driving by with their headlights on. She moved to the front door, opened it, stepped out on the porch, took a deep breath of the cool breeze, and surveyed the neighbors inside their darkened houses snugly sleeping.

She stepped back into her house, closed the door, turned, seeing the old couple sitting there expectantly, and returned to her seat at the table.

"By a door!" she growled.

"I know this is a lot to absorb right now, but we have already gone back once and failed. We cannot do it again unless you come too," Hans repeated.

"Why do I have to come, assuming I don't really know what you mean by this 'door'?"

"Because you are an adult who was born in 1981. You will remain an adult when we go back, but we will not. Carl, Lian, Ada, Clotilda, and I will be children just like we were then. We can do so much, but we must have an adult. A person who can work in front of us, and be the one to deal with other adults. Children, alone, can achieve nothing that we need to do," again Hans pleaded.

Cully put both hands on the table in front of her. Then she asked patiently, "What do you mean 'then' and 'you will be children'?"

"Cully," said Clotilda in her sincerest voice, "we are talking about returning to 1942, when we were children. It is the only way we can save them: the two girls. Mina was 10 at the time, and D'avia was 11. This was the point in time we met D'avia. We already knew Mina. We became part of their lives, and their struggle to survive. We need to help them. Our lives and memories depend on it. I know you are going to think us crazy. But we are not, and if you believe in a God you cannot see, then you need to believe in us. This is real, and it took us such a long time to find you. Can you understand this?"

28

Clotilda looked like she had tears in her eyes, as did Hans, when he turned his head away to cough.

Cully starred at each one going between them like watching a tennis match. She lowered her head and spoke, "Surely, you must understand that this is too fantastic a story for me to believe. Surely, you can't be serious. Return to 1942 Germany. I've never been, I mean this isn't real."

She looked at them again, and both Hans and Clotilda put a hand on each of Cullies' hands. She felt a surprising warmth that enveloped her from their touch. Then she whispered, "I just, I just…. this is crazy."

"I know, mein Liebster," Clotilda said sympathetically without withdrawing her had. "Dear one."

Cully sat and remained speechless for several minutes, during which neither elderly individual spoke. They just waited with their hands on Cully's.

"I have to sleep," Cully said calmly, "in my own bed. I have to think while I'm in that bed. I may not really get any sleep. But I need you to leave now, please. I can't absorb this whole concept." She looked up; they removed their hands from hers and she felt the comforting sensation vanish immediately. That unsettled her.

Hans and Clotilda rose from their seats, walked toward the door, turned and met Cully's gaze while she was still seated at the dining table. She was at a loss for words. She pursed her lips, and just nodded. The two elderly people turned to leave. Clotilda turned briefly and said, "You have a birthmark, a reddish-brown mole right below your throat where a necklace might hang. She turned and followed Hans out the door.

Cully did not move for a few minutes, then rose from her chair and walked to her bedroom as if in a daze. Once in her bedroom, she disrobed and put on her nightgown as if in a trance. The whole time, she had her brow wrinkled, and her mouth was a perfect 'O' of astonishment. She pulled her

29

comforter back, and got into bed looking down at the mole that had been covered up till now. Nestling down into her pillow, she spoke out loud to herself,

"Through a door!?" She knew she wouldn't sleep a wink that night but would instead concentrate on mulling over what happened, what was said, who these people were, what they wanted, how incredible it was what they were telling her…and she felt exhausted into a deep sleep.

# Chapter VI

Cully got up the next day feeling somewhat tired still, but well enough for a day of work. However, while drinking her morning latte, she pondered going into work with everything that happened the night before. She sucked on her upper lip, a bad habit when she concentrated on a thought. Decidedly, she went to find her cellphone in the bedroom, called into work and told them she was not feeling well at all, suggested it might be food poisoning to make it sound more authentic.

She then put on her robe, dropped her cellphone on her bed, closed the bedroom door, and went to the couch, picking up the T.V. remote before she sat down. Since Cully did not have the closeness with her siblings to talk to or discuss things with, she sometimes felt sorry for herself and lonely. The kinds of things she wanted to discuss she would not do so with her children. They were far too young and not what she considered her peers. Her few friends at work were dealing with their own stuff, and she wasn't close enough to anybody who might not think she was bonkers. The remote in her hand, the T.V. turned on, she put on YouTube, and watch her favorite clips of *Britain's Got Talent*, America's Got Talent, and clips of *The Voice* from all over the world. She loved watching the contestants being supported by their excited family members. She smiled as singer after singer showed excitement when they received his or her dream of getting all 'yeses' from the judges to move onto the next round. Truly, she invested her emotions in these programs, and they temporarily made her feel happy.

After a few hours of watching YouTube, Cully clicked off the T.V. and sat hugging a pillow, straining her brain to figure out how to feel about those elderly people, what they proposed, what was so incredible about the whole thing. She made a mental list of pros and cons her husband had taught her to do when they were first married when facing any decision of great import. Okay, she tried to think logically, *pros: adventure, doing something inconceivable like visiting 1942 and being in Europe during the war first hand, experiencing a fantasy, actually saving someone's life? Cons, she thought, ending up in a bad place or predicament, getting hurt physically or dying. If she tries this, people will think she's crazy, she will end up in a mental institution, or she will get lost in another era she can't come back from. Yeah, she thought, that about sums it up. But how those people touched her! She felt a real difference when they did that, and an even bigger one when they withdrew their hands. How is that possible, she wondered.*

Cully could just ignore it like a bad dream, except for the part about saving two little girls from harm. They seemed so convincing, but it's crazy! Cully got up and threw the pillow at a lamp knocking it over with anger. "Why me!" she yelled. Standing in the middle of the living room, hand on hip, she covered her face with her hand and thought about *magicians like David Copperfield and the train car of people he made vanish, Criss Angel and the poster he rubbed on a store window until it was on the other side of the glass in front of teenage witnesses, for crying out loud! These were all things that Cully felt were impossible, yet verified by witnesses. Of course, these guys don't explain to anyone how they do these things, but still, no one, so far as she knew, could truly imagine how they were done. And, time travel! What about that? Maybe there really is magic in the world, and the few people who know it are keeping it a well-guarded secret.* She further pondered, standing in the middle of the living room still. *It could be like*

32

*that movie, Chain Reaction, where the characters invented a safe, clean form of hydrogen energy that they were keeping from the Congress that funded the research. Maybe there really is a program messing with time travel.* She remembered an article she read about Einstein's theory of the 'space-time continuum. *Everything was relative to your viewpoint.*

Finally, Cully got tired of her indecision. Then, again, if she does this, she could get hurt or worse disappear. What about her children? *Oh, I don't know…*she thought frustratingly. Cully picked up the fallen lamp, and plopped back down on the couch. She had lost so much in her life. Her beautiful boy, Byron, her father too early, an adult relationship with her siblings, and her mother's death over which she never cried. She was lonely and sad, and felt sorry for herself, a feeling she hated more than anything. Taking a deep breath, she vowed to listen to more of what the old couple wanted her to go through. She was at a not-so-good point in her life where she was willing to take a crazy risk and see what their fantasy involved. After all, she thought, *she could just stop at any point if she wasn't comfortable. Ooops! How was she going to get in touch with them?* She didn't know. She shot over to the front window and looked out. Nothing, no one on the sidewalk. She went and whipped open her front door. Nothing, no one on the porch. Now she felt ridiculously disappointed! She yelled to the air, "Damn! I choose to do this insane thing, and I don't even know how to get in touch with them."

# Chapter VII

**J**ust as Cully was going toward her bedroom to change into her sweats for the rest of the day, the doorbell rang. She stood still to make sure she heard it. *Yep, there it was again*; she heard it, so she freshly wrapped her robe around herself and headed for the door. Upon opening it, there was a gentleman in a post office type suit.

"Hello, madam. Telegram for you," he held it out to her. Cully looked at him in wonder, then at his hand, and asked,

"A telegram? Who still gets telegrams," she asked slowly.

"Oh, jeez," he said, "people still send telegrams, ma'am, just not as much, usually it's for money."

"So, it's like Western Union, here I come," Cully mimicked from an old commercial.

The delivery guy looked at her backing his head away, "Ah, no, it's International Telegram. Pretty much like Western Union."

Cully, immediately, felt stupid and embarrassed. "So sorry, I just never received a telegram in like my whole life." She stared at the telegram window and her name and address listed. She began to open it, but realized the guy was still standing there. She asked, "Am I supposed to tip you or something?"

"Well, even though one never came to you 'like never in your whole life', it is considered appropriate for a hand-delivered telegram," he replied formally.

Cully backed up to her hall table behind her still staring at the telegram, and grabbed a five-dollar bill from the blue bowl on the end. She reached out to him without looking at him and said, "Thank you." The deliveryman, happy with his tip, repeated the words to her, turned and left for his truck. Cully closed the door absently. She moved to the couch once again, and found her letter opener on the side table. She gently put it in the end of the telegraph and slit it open. She hesitated a moment, then opened the envelope and withdrew the telegram with two fingers as if it would bite her. She tried to read it from her two-finger hold, but failing to do so, finally opened it with her whole hand and read:

*C:*

*Please meet us at the Harbinger Tavern in Chicago at 1520 N. Damien Avenue, precisely at 5pm. You need to walk beside The Chicago Hotel and down the alley. It is poorly lit, but halfway down there is a red door with iron cross-hatching on it. Knock twice. A small window in the door will open. Say to the person who opens it, the word, 'library'. She will not speak to you. She will just open the door. We will be seated at a round table on the second level down, left, from the door. I will stand, so you know where to go directly. Please, do not tell anyone you are coming.*

*Hans*

Besides the fact that Cully was astonished to get a telegram, she realized it was already 3p.m. So, she stopped trying to. She walked to her bedroom, got ready to go out in jeans, a teal-colored top, her leather jacket, and her knit hat that she always wore out. Cully rushed down through the house, grabbed her purse, opened and slammed the door, and walked swiftly to her car.

# Chapter VIII

She stood at the corner of The Chicago Hotel as if she were waiting for a ride. The sidewalk was busy with foot traffic going to and from in front of her. She did not look anyone in the eyes. Gradually, Cully would move her feet a few more inches toward the alley. She glanced down the alley once and saw the building wall with its corners and angles resembling a corrugated roof. Each angle delved deeper into the shadows of the alley. She, finally, rolled her shoulder around the corner into the shadow of the building when she felt that nobody was watching. Cully moved slowly down the alley, walking backward at times to make sure no one was following her. She was wholly unaccustomed to frequenting alleys as part of her life experience in the city. Thus, she was a little anxious. What ran through her mind were all the movies where people were either dragged or hiding in blind alleys and bad things happened. She tried to shrug off the chill of her nervousness, and surreptitiously turned around making her way down the alley while gliding her right hand over the brick wall. Two more angles down, she saw the red door as Hans had described it. Cully stood in front of the door, fist raised to knock, but she froze. She contemplated running back to the safety of the sidewalk, and, wondering what the hell she was doing. The thought that this was all too weird had not left her mind. As she took slow deep breaths to relax herself, she decided that she would fight her fear. She knocked twice.

It seemed to take forever before the little window in the door opened, and a rather attractive old woman peered at her with no expression on her face. Cully paused; the woman waited; Cully slowly and clearly said the word 'library' to which the window softly closed and the door opened just wide enough to admit Cully. The attractive, old woman wore a plain gray blouse, a black skirt that hung below her knees, a grayish apron tied around her waist, and black oxford shoes that matched her stockings. Cully took all this in within seconds, so the woman would not think she was staring. As Cully turned, she was enveloped in a fog of cigarette and cigar smoke, which threatened to make her choke, so she covered her nose with her hat. However, strangely, the smell changed into a pleasant scent. It smelled of men puffing on pipes with a rich scent of tobacco. She always like the scent of pipe smoking.

The old woman held her hand out to indicate Cully was to enter further into the darkened room, so she moved forward slowly, noticing groups of people at various tables set up in alcoves. Oddly, she saw that no one was paying her any attention but ensconced in murmured conversations among their groups. She headed forward slowly, since Hans had said the "second level down" from the door, not wanting to fall on her face. However, Hans met her at the second landing indicating two stressed wood railings that she could use to step down the six steps to the next level. Hans smiled at her but did not speak. He took her hand as if she were being brought to a dance floor and guided her to a large round table, in an ample alcove, around which sat five people. There were three men and two women. She recognized the woman she had seen with Hans before, still immaculately dressed. The other woman and men were dressed like Hans and Ada. Cully felt like she was in *Twilight Zone*, but tried to control her reaction with her silence. She looked at Hans for guidance, and he indicated a chair she was to sit in. She lowered herself into the chair, slowly, trying not to smile, but look cordial. Hans immediately introduced the group.

"Cully, you remember Ada Frietag from our previous meeting. Then we have, Clotilda Kappel, my last name is Obermardt, and this is Klaus Gerhardt to my left; and this young man", Hans said cheerfully about a genial-looking man, "is Lian Kurtz."

Cully starred at Clotilda to which Clotilda just winked at her. Cully felt embarrassed and looked down. Hans asked, "Is anything the matter, Cully?"

Cully raised her head and explained, "I'll be honest with you. I'm incredibly nervous and feel very strange being here."

Hans replied, "Cully, you are among people who only care about you. What seems odd to you, you should try to dismiss. We are aware this all seems very clandestine to you. But, after we explain the situation, trust me, you will feel perhaps a little stranger. We will take it slow. Just remember to breathe to try to calm yourself. You are in no danger here, I assure you. Quite the contrary, your safety is of primary concern to us."

With that Cully relaxed a bit, and Hans asked if she would like some water. He offered nothing else despite the fact that all the others looked as if they were drinking beer in steins. Again, it appeared an old-fashion scene from a movie. However, she nodded her head, and said, "I would love water, and I do not need ice, thank you." He chuckled, "Well, good, water it is, and we, actually, have no ice here."

Water was delivered to the table in the form of a pitcher and a heavy glass. Hans poured for her. She drank slowly but for a whole thirty seconds assuaging her apprehensive thirst. Once finished, Cully said, "Thank you, Hans. That was good."

Hans replied, "You are most welcome, Cully. Now, we must tell you a story. It is very important you do not interrupt. Although, here is a paper and a pencil for you to write down any questions you may have. Please save them for when we are done speaking."

Once again, Cully nodded her head, took the paper and unmarked pencil, and made herself as comfortable as she could in her chair to listen. She leaned forward on the table as she often did to give close attention to a speaker. There was a pause at the table for, perhaps, a moment. Each individual glanced at each other, before Clotilda began.

"As I already met you, Cully, I will begin, hopefully to put you a little at ease. But, we will all take turns to speak. Please try to relax and just listen. Do not predict anything from what we tell you. That will be explained. Do you think you can do that?"

"Yes," Cully said, trying to relax and listen closely.

# Chapter IX

"In 1942, World War II was raging through Europe. It was a big stage. However, it was the little stages that built the big stage. A young girl named Mina Engel lived in Stuttgart, Germany. Her father was the tower controller in the railroad yard. It was called the 'round house' even though it was a rectangle. I think because he could see trains and tracks from all sides of the tower. It was a large, three-story structure of which the top floor was the tower, and a small house occupied the other two floors. The tower had large, slanted windows from the roof to half-way down the whole top floor. It is so he could see if anyone was hiding by the walls below him, or were not where they were supposed to be across tracks. This yard was one of many to which the Germans were herding Jews and dissidents to await deportation to concentration camps. Perhaps you have heard of the term 'death camps?'" Ada asked.

Cully nodded, but did not speak. Klaus continued, "Mina was terribly abused by her mother. Her mother and father fought quite a bit, and her mother would take it out on Mina. She would hit her, burn her with the iron, or make her do chores all day, some of which were very difficult for a 10-year-old girl. Mina was slight in her build because her mother would not give her a great deal to eat. Oh, she fed her enough, but only because when the inspector came to check on her father, her mother wanted Mina to smile as if she was a healthy German child. She needed to appear convinced that

41

the Jews were the problem in a strong German society. He would ask her questions regularly, as he asked her parents. They displayed a fierce loyalty to him. But, Mina was not." Cully leaned in closer because she wanted to clearly hear what Klaus meant by this statement. However, Lian Kurtz took over explaining. He was sitting next to Cully, so she turned, sat back in her chair, and gave Lian her full attention.

Lian continued, "Mina was an amazing young girl. Despite what she went through with her mother, her father adored her but ignored her for the most part. She accomplished something only a few people were brave enough to do in Germany at the time. She hid a little Jewess. She was eleven-years-old. Her name was D'avia Schulenburg. However, Mina tried to get her to the Swiss border three times on the train, which proved to be too much of a challenge for a young girl. It met with failure after failure," Lian paused, staring at air, then "They always had to turn back because they faced obstacles that children did not have the experience, cleverness, nor knowledge to overcome! The German train stops at the border of Switzerland, and one has to board the Swiss train to travel further. Do not mistake me. Mina was very courageous in hiding this little girl. D'avia was very grateful, but she saw the hardship it was taking on Mina. She did not know what to do; she loved Mina so, like a sister. When the mother of Mina, suspected something and followed Mina into the woods one day where Mina had built her 'bunker', as she called it. Although, her mother followed her only so far because, she was too anxious to go further, as the trees became dense the further, she went in. She was a very nervous woman. Entering too deeply into the woods was just one more thing she feared."

Then, across the table, Clotilda took over the narrative, "Her mother called the German State Security. She told them that, as sad as she was, she was a loyal German citizen and was afraid her daughter was hiding someone in the woods near the train tracks." She stared into Cully's eyes. "She turned in her own daughter!" Clotilda paused at this point, and wetness appeared in her eyes. She sniffled, got her handkerchief out to wipe her nose, and then resumed talking, "The SS came out quickly, with dogs and followed the mother's directions as to where she thought Mina ran off to. The State Security Police combed the area for a few hours with sticks, thrusting them into any pile of leaves or branches on the ground. They were like dogs, themselves, straining at their collars going further into the woods. Eventually…," At this point, Clotilda could not finish, and Klaus covered Clotilda's hand with his and took over, "Eventually, as well built as Mina's bunker was, one security soldier suspected something. It bothered him enough that he returned to an area passed a big log surrounded by bushes on the ground that hid the opening to Mina's bunker. He had to sweep aside heavy branches, leaves, and an old board to get down and put his head through the door to their hide-out and found the two girls," At which point, Ada took over, "I suppose you can imagine what happened. But I will tell you. The Jewess, D'avia was taken directly to the trains and transported to the concentration camp at Flossenbeurg."

Cully bent forward and covered her face. She asked, "Please tell me what happened to Mina. Quickly."

Hans placed his warm hand on her back for a gesture of support. He made a small bow. "An hour after they found the girls, Mina was shot in front of her parents." Cully squeezed her eyes shut. "Apparently, the SS believed the parents had nothing to do with hiding the girl, particularly because of the value of her father's job, but it was meant as a warning. Her mother had little reaction, but her father wept openly and viciously slapped his wife.

Cully was beside herself. She remained dry-eyed much to her surprise. She sat up and asked, "Why are you telling me this horrible story?" She tried to muster up anger at these people who brought her here simply to tell her a sad story. "Why am I here?" Cully asked with a hush.

The five people, so impeccably dressed in the clothes of another era, turned to her avoiding her eyes. Klaus, finally raised his head and reported, "You can help us save both girls."

Cully looked at Klaus, dropping her mouth open, "How in the world can I save children that are dead? What are they spirits or zombies or what? This sounds insane." She paused and thought, "There is more to this, isn't there? There is something you think I can do, or you would not be telling me this."

Ada replied, "You are correct, Cully, but you will be afraid. I want you to know that. You will not want to believe us, despite the fact that there is something very important you can do. It will be dangerous, and, for that reason, we need you to hear what you can do, and how, and think. We would not be asking you, if some strong English or American soldier could do this. Or, if the underground patriots could have smuggled them to safety. It must be you. Only you can change what happened."

Cully got up from her seat and said, "I have to use the restroom. I hope there is one in here."

"Of course," answered Klaus. He pointed down two more shallow levels, and told her to turn right. Cully, in a daze, tried to focus on the steps, so she wouldn't fall. She got to the bottom, and immediately forgot which way to go. She turned left. Before she could take two steps, a strange, elderly, woman was at her side, grabbed her arm firmly, and turned her around.

"This way, my dear." The woman was dressed in clean, modest clothing of what Cully guessed would be common in an eatery from a past decade. She gently pulled her arm away from the woman, and proceeded to the correct door.

Cully relieved herself, and crossed to wash her hands at the sink. The bathroom looked like any other bathroom in an old Chicago building with single sinks and exposed plumbing. It was clean though. She looked at

44

herself in the discolored mirror. She stared at herself not comprehending the bizarre situation she was in. Finally, someone knocked on the door and asked if she was all right. Cully blurted, "Yes! I'm just washing my hands." Below her, the sink sparkled. She turned on the cold water, bent over, and splashed her face with abundant amounts of water. It splashed on her everywhere. She didn't care. She stopped suddenly, realizing she was very wet: top, sleeves, and pants. She suddenly felt stupid and took actual towels from the counter and tried vigorously to wipe herself dry.

Again, came the gentle knock. "Cully, dear, are you sure you are all right?" Cully stood silent for a few seconds, then said, "No, not really."

"May I come in?" It was Ada.

"Sure, come on in."

Ada entered the restroom quietly and approached Cully. She extended her hand to Cully's elbow as if to support it.

"A little overwhelming, Cully?"

"That would be a mild way of putting it."

"We expected that. Here drink this. It will help with your nerves," Ada said as she offered her a shot glass with an amber liquid in it. "All at once, Cully."

Cully followed her instructions and threw it down her throat briskly, then blew out her breath through her mouth coughing and demanded, "What was that?!"

Ada ignored her question and asked, with an accommodating smile, "Are you ready to go sit down? Were you able to dry off your clothes enough?"

Cully looked at her quizzically because it startled her that Ada was so gracious in how she asked her the last question, as if what Cully did was not a surprise to her.

# Chapter X

Once reseated, Cully bent forward with trepidation.

"Okay, so as I asked before, what can I do to change this story?"

Hans looked at her with a crinkly-eyed smile, "I know you are afraid. We expected that. You would not be a sane person if you were not afraid. But we will be there to protect you as much as we can. We will shadow you in a way that others cannot see us. What I said before; the girls almost made it to Switzerland twice, but had to turn around. The reason is we need an adult to coordinate the change of events from what happened." He paused. "This is what you are afraid of, and let me reassure you it is real. We are going to take you back to 1942. Truly, we have done it once before. We are not crazy, but, of course, you are going to think we are crazy because we mentioned to you 'by way of using a door'."

"Yes," Cully said, "that was what I thought you said. "It sounds like science fiction theater, psychoanalysis-pick one."

Clotilda interjected, "Cully, this is where you have to let go of your reality and have faith in ours. Quite a tall order, I know. But, if you do not want to do this, we will understand. You are our last hope."

"But, what of my siblings?" Cully interrupted. "They are also of my heritage, blood, whatever ties me to this, for lack of a better word, a scary, bizarre adventure."

Here Klaus hummed, and held up his finger to the group, continuing, "Cully, your siblings are not like you. We studied you. We considered Sybil, Jack, and F.J. Isn't that what you call him? They do not have what you have, Cully, that is needed to help us."

All five of the elderly group looked at her with kindly smiles. But Hans was the first to speak, "Cully, we eliminated them because they are all static personalities who still carry grudges from the past that continue to consume them."

"Static? I don't quite understand."

Klaus turned to look at Cully sitting next to him, "Cully, your brother, Joseph, is a wounded soul, who has not revealed to you the disappointment he hides beneath the surface of his demeanor. The disappointment is in him. He and his inner conflicts concerning your father and his own insecurities have never been resolved. He has never evolved into the person you are."

Lian continued, "Cully, Jack and Sybil do not possess a natural empathy for anyone. They are highly structured and attempt to control every situation, encounter, or family gathering. They continue to be saddled with their own invasive needs that also have not been addressed, nor deconstructed. And no one can help them because they are not willing to exchange what they perceive as wrongs done to them in the past by some person for the unknown possibility of an unburdened life. Sybil, especially, would never take the risk to move forward. She is too frightened of anything different from the routine she has established for many years. And Jack, well, Jack tells himself that he is on top of the world in his life. He is, possibly, the saddest of them all because he thinks he is the best of all of you. When, in fact, he is the least stable of all of Adele's children.

Cully stared, dumfounded, at the group. Her eyes slid back and forth, left to right, scanning their faces. They looked normal, like they had not just parted with information that was astute, evaluating her siblings as individuals. She asked in a croak, "How do you know all this?" Then she cleared her throat and repeated, "How would you know all this? Have you met my sister and brothers?"

This time Klaus gently covered her hand with his warmth, the same warmth that she had experienced before. "Mein Lebling, we know this. That is all we can tell you. How we know it, is not important, if we are successful in this operation for lack of a better word. When it came to you, we breathed a sigh of relief. We knew we had found the right person. We discovered that you are very different from all of your siblings. You let yourself grow. You do not dwell on the hurts of the past but move forward in life. You learned from others how to handle challenging situations. You read books to help you figure out the best ways to work around difficult people. You love children because you have so much love to give. Most importantly, you are, and always will be, a nurturer and a person who cannot stop helping, loving, giving, and caring for other people. You consider it a fault in you that you would like to turn off because you think it has caused you so much pain in your life. But it is what makes your life rich. In fact, you don't even consider it as a choice in your life, which is why you are exactly what we need. You are an empath in its truest form. Despite all the things that have happened to you that could have turned you into an unforgiving person, the empath qualities you possess and the nurturing nature are and always will be core to who you are. Because of this you are very strong which inspires us to ask you to be a part of this."

Cully felt tears on her face. She was no longer confused, but decided to have faith in these people. Perhaps, because they said all the things Cully wanted to believe or feel. She let go of her pragmatism. She felt she was in the presence of a family, yet it still did not clearly make sense. Although, she felt an oddly serene confidence. She scanned the faces again, and spoke, "It no longer matters what you want me to do. I will abandon asking for explanations for now. I will try to remain calm when you tell me what it has to do with this door. I choose to have faith in you."

49

The entire group of elderly figures smiled at her. They rose from the table and told her they needed to move to another room to explain the plan and her essential role. As the individuals got up, they raised their glasses to each other. Cully followed suit with her water, and together, the six of them said, "God bless us all."

They followed each other down an additional two levels, with Cully in the middle, and turned left at the bottom level. She saw a seven-step staircase leading down to an old but sturdy door padlocked at shoulder level. Hans brought out a key and opened the lock, secured the padlock and opened the door for Cully. She entered the room, observing an old table and three benches in the center of a small room. The room was darkly paneled, heavily speckled with age. To her right were several wardrobes against the wall from what looked like the Victorian era. They appeared to be well-maintained antiques.

After the five people gave Cully a couple of minutes to look around the room, Hans began to talk to her.

"Cully, in these wardrobes are clothing appropriate for 1942. You will have to change into an outfit from that era. You will have a suitcase packed with a few more outfits in them. We have sufficient Reichsmarks for you to acquire other things and transportation."

"What are Reichsmarks?" Cully asked, "I thought Deutsche Marks were used in Germany?"

"Not until 1948, Cully," answered Hans.

"Oh, I know my history for the most part, but not that tidbit," she replied.

Ada commented, "Yes, we know you love history, and this will be most helpful."

Hans continued, "Once we are properly clothed, we will discuss a few details of a plan that we have and look at a map of Germany more specifically the area between Stuttgart and Switzerland. The Swiss have guards across their borders cutting anyone off from Germany. In fact, there was a little traffic between Switzerland and Germany during the war. Both Swiss and Germans could cross the border roads with special permission, but not all Germans were admitted. It depended on their papers and the reason they wanted to enter the country. Most Swiss who crossed had relatives in the countryside and were permitted to visit them, as long as they were not Jewish. However, there is no record of any successful attempt by Jewish people to cross the border at the roadhouse gate. I'm afraid that they would have been turned away as Switzerland was determined to stay neutral in the eyes of the world during this second war conflict, and a portion of them were anti-Semitic.

However, we will eat first, then dress and discuss. You must be sure not to have anything on you from after 1942. We will keep your current things here, and the ladies will look you over and ask questions. You can ask them questions too that might be of a personal nature. Does that sound all right?"

Cully nodded her head and took a seat at one of the benches Lian and Klaus had dragged around to the table. Clotilda brought out a large map from somewhere. She folded the map twice and placed it at the end of the table. What seemed like out of nowhere, a stout waiter with a long white, waist apron brought platters of food he placed on the table. Plates and glasses of beer were placed in front of each person. Cully turned to see where he went. She had been too preoccupied to see how he entered the room. She assumed it was through the door the group entered, but then one of the wardrobes opened, and the waiter emerged into the room bringing out large cloth napkins. Once dispensed, he left through the wardrobe, closing the door behind him. Ada smiled at Cully, "We will have to teach you how to control your facial expressions. You give away too much with your face."

# Chapter XI

After eating a stable meal (the dishes having been cleared by the mysterious waiter), the group surrounded the table standing and leaning over the map Clotilda had lying on the table. It was a map of Stuttgart flowing over to the Black Forest continuing to Switzerland's border, as well as Austria-Hungary's, France's, Yugoslavia's and several other countries that suffered during the German invasions.

Klaus pointed his finger to Stuttgart, "Have you ever heard of this city in Germany?"

"Yes," Cully replied. "I know my European history of major cities at that time."

"Good!" Klaus continued. "this is where Mina lives with her parents on the west side by the railroad yards. Their home is actually beneath the observation tower so that her father can view all of the activity by the station and the adjacent buildings, including several two-story factories. He is in communication with the Germans by a dedicated telephone when they bring the Jews to the platform for transporting to the concentration camps. I think you know about most of this?"

"Yes, I am familiar with the process of exporting the Jews."

"Good! You are going to be most valuable with your knowledge. Now, the overall plan is to get Mina and D'avia from their hideout through the

Black Forest and into Switzerland over land, little use of roads. It is 105 kilometers to the Black Forest, or 68 miles for your American benefit. You need to begin thinking in kilometers."

"I can do that," Cully said with confident care.

Lian took over the explanation, "Then it is 242 kilometers to the Swiss border, or 150 miles. You will be using any transportation we can find, and you will be walking a bit. It will not be an easy journey for a woman traveling with seven small children. We will help you with as much transportation as is safe, but know this. It is going to take your ingenuity to make the hard and dangerous trip easier, and you must take great precaution. To that end, you will be first spending at least a month in Stuttgart first."

"A month? Why so long?" Cully raised her brow.

"Because we have to work with you on a daily basis and train you to get a job, to establish yourself as a person that is strategically placed, but invisible in looks and nature to the people around you. We want to get information from you to help us, but we also need you to look like a person most people in an office would pay little attention to. Understand?"

"Yes, I think I do," Cully said while nodding her head.

At this point Ada continued prepping Cully with an explanation of the activities she would have to engage in to establish her persona non-grata. Then Clotilda answered questions of a personal nature for a woman living in the era of the war. While Hans gave her the pertinent details of how Cully would observe Mina's mother. She was told that she would watch her from a distance to sense the things that set her off on a tirade. She had no visitors. The Mother was often outside hanging wash or tending her little garden. Thus, Cully would know what to expect from her behavior, but warned to not get too close. For She would get suspicious and begin asking too many questions. Cully was instructed to be wary of the father completely. He was suspicious of anyone who came to his home, or he saw on the train platform,

53

tracks, or anywhere near the train cars. Especially, a woman would draw attention anywhere he had a view from his arena post. Next, Hans discussed with Cully the type of job she needed to apply for. They wanted her to work in a military office in Stuttgart, preferably as a secretary for a middle level officer. The reason was that top secretaries were too conspicuous and often socialized with senior personnel.

"A middle level officer can be very valuable because they often have access to valuable information with which they do nothing. They don't have enough power, and they frequently don't even know how valuable the information is. They manage workers in the office, attend meetings because they are a part of the senior officer's staff, but ask only questions about their specific assignments, clerical staff organization, and average day-to-day business of the office. However, in this particular office, there are senior officers that manage departments, and are a more vocal part of the staff for the highest-ranking officer."

"So, who is the highest-ranking officer?"

Klaus continued to inform her, "In this office, it is a *Mitarbeiter* we want you to work for. You can consider him like a colonel to you. He would be commanded by a *Dienstleiter,* a high-level officer or what you might consider a general. He is very important politically, and this one rules the government office in Stuttgart at this time. But he could be promoted to Berlin. We just don't know, so you have to be very careful to be invisible to him as much as possible. You know what I mean by invisible?"

Cully answered, "I believe so. You mean like wear glasses, dress in a brown-colored skirt, with a beige blouse, and wear your hair in a severe style so as not to draw any attention to yourself? Keep your head down, and never look any of the officers in the eye."

Ada commented, "You are already knowledgeable of the little things which make a difference. But you will be wearing a uniform, very bland. Good, Clotilda."

"Please, please, my name is Cully," she pleaded with her.

"I am so sorry. Of course, you are Cully."

Lian spoke, "I will be the one to help you get a secretarial position for a *Mitarbeiter.*"

"How will you do that?" Cully questioned.

Lian answered abruptly, "You must not ask any more of those types of questions. You need to have faith in us that we can do what we say."

Clotilda patted his arm, "Lian, think about how she sees this whole task. Be patient with her."

"I know, I know. I am sorry."

Cully raised her eyebrows and stated, "One problem. I don't know how to speak German. I don't know how to even pronounce those words you spoke naming the officers, nor do I know what 'Dehna' means."

All five looked at her for a moment, and Ada said, "Dehna means dear one. The words used to describe the officer's positions will not be a problem. We can do this, put you into 1942; you can speak what you hear as English, but to the others, it will come out in German. And..," she paused when she saw the look on Cully's face, her eyes opening wide. "When they speak to you, you will hear it in English. However, even in English, your tone must be clipped and formal. Also, you can refer to the officers simply as 'Herr this' and 'Herr' that.

Cully stared at the five figures. "How is that possible?"

"How is this whole venture possible?" Hans retorted.

"I don't know, but it is already so fantasy like, you want me to just have faith?"

"Exactly. We cannot explain to you anything right now. I don't know that you would believe us. And we have to do this, and we need you to just do what we ask. Questions about what we want you to do are all right, but we just cannot tell you why. Please don't ask right now. The answer will come in time, but I'm afraid not until the girls are safely in Switzerland."

Then Cully inquired throwing her hands up, "Ok, but one question. Where am I taking the girls to? What is the destination in Switzerland?"

Ada once again chimed in, "We do not know yet. But, do not worry. Your job is to help us get them to Switzerland, and then there we will find answers."

Cully sat down in a position like *The Thinker* statue in the Chicago Museum. She was quiet. The quieter she stayed, the more anxious the group became. They glanced at her and then each other. They began showing anxiety on their faces. Cully looked up at them,

"What's the matter?"

Clotilda said slowly, "You look like you're changing your mind, and feeling doubtful about this?"

Cully hesitantly answered, "Oh, no, it's alright. I just have to surrender any sense of reality in the next month."

Lian bent down, and quietly said to Cully, "When you are there, it will be reality, just one that is different than you are used to. It will be real, Cully. If you are not careful as we help you, you could end up in trouble and get stuck there. Your children would never have been born. Do you understand? I'm not trying to scare you, but what you are about to undertake is very real. Are you having second thoughts? We would understand if you were. We would be sad, but we would understand. We will bring you back, that is a promise I am going to make you!"

Cully scanned their faces looking at them all, these people that lived through World War II and in Germany. She couldn't imagine what it must have been like. But she often wondered about what she would have done if she had lived back then. She had studied much about the rise of Hitler, the apathy of the elite citizens of Germany and even some of the public who were aware, the ignorance of or even non-belief of the many who had no idea what Hitler was doing with the Jews, the overwhelming fear that grew among the people in Berlin, and the ability of the soldiers who could turn away from a previous caring personality and become so instantly cruel to people. Jews or not, when you looked them in the eyes, they were people, for which the soldiers discarded any sense of morality and made them suffer by beating and killing them because of their faith. They slapped children to the ground, shot them, and most horrifically shot whole families if they had any trouble from them. That bit she actually remembered from a holocaust survivor she was interviewing years ago for her thesis, the final college paper. Martha. That was her name. The woman wept during part of the interview. She had said it was like yesterday that she could vividly remember the atrocities committed. She, herself, was on the train station platform when she witnessed a few officers who shot children for causing trouble. She could still see the mother today; it never left her.

Cully remembered hugging the woman after the interview while Cully cried with this elderly woman. Cully knew, as ridiculous as it seemed, she had to do this, to help these people. Perhaps, she would save only two lives, but that would be something, more than accepting what happened to those girls. She couldn't bear thinking about their fate if she didn't try. She abandoned her feeling of loss she experienced in her life. She felt an overwhelming purpose.

# Chapter XII

She began to dress in her proper attire. Cully was provided with oxford shoes, heavy stockings, a dark gray skirt, a white blouse buttoned to her neck and a small black tie. The uniform had a pouchy hat for her head and all the emblems necessary for her clothes. She was also provided with two pairs of glasses. One clear, one with a non-descript prescription in them in case anyone asked to see her glasses. She was to carry both pairs at all times. She was given a long wool coat suitable for the end of winter the year she was entering. She was provided with gloves. Ada told her that she would only get one pair, so she needed to take care of them. Her hair was pulled back into a style of the time, which Ada had to do because Cully was bewildered by how the unfamiliar hairstyle was achieved.

The five gave her a basic black purse with a long strap. She was allowed to put a handkerchief, lipstick, matches, cigarettes, a cheap compact, and a comb into it along with identity papers.

"I won't even ask where you got the identity papers," Cully quipped. "Don't they do background checks?" Cully turned and asked the group.

Ada smiled mischievously.

Ada answered, "The uniform will speak for itself. They don't have the time, and if you tell them, you have little family, they will be not suspicious at all. You will be what you are today, although, don't stand out with your skills too strongly, curb your self-initiative. Also, you will get used to a typewriter."

After this conversation, and Cully finishing dressing, putting on a coat to top off her outfit, the group began to dress. Now, Cully was once again surprised. She really did not understand this.

"Okay, this is really odd," she commented, pointing at the group, "why are you dressing in children's clothing? I need an answer to that one."

Clotilda smiled patiently, "Cully, do you think we could do much as we are?"

Hans continued, "Ok, sit down. Remember about having faith?"

Cully stood and raised her voice, "No, no, not this one. Tell me now!"

The entire group encouraged her to sit down and then surrounded her in a standing, semi-circle. Klaus sat next to Cully and spoke calmly, "Cully, we were children in 1942." He let it sink in to her thoughts, and then, surprisingly she said, "Of course you would be!" I can go back as myself, right? Because I didn't exist, but you did. So you have to go back to the age you were. Is that right?"

Klaus clapped his hands, "Yes, Cully, you have it!"

"But, how will you help me if you are children?"

Klaus looked at Lian and Hans and Ada and Clotilda and sighed.

Ada came to Cully's knees and looked down at her face, "We lived, we watched, we were all quite smart, so we were 'let's say' gifted children. We will be able to help you most of the way, and if we can't, we will tell you what to do. We will always be around you somewhere. Okay? We are very clever, and we have a great deal of knowledge passed on to us."

Cully smiled up at Ada, "I wish I had had a mother like you. It is my great sadness, my mother being the way she was. If we asked whether we

59

had any relatives beyond her, she was so dismissive. She would always just tell us 'They're all dead' and discourage any further question of the matter."

"What you are doing is a miracle, Cully, so you never know what miracles you can make happen for others. Is that good enough?"

Cully looked down at her hands, silent.

Lian looked at his watch, "We need to go now. It's time. Cully, remember to keep your watch on you at all times. I can carry one and say it is my father's, but the rest of the group cannot. It would look suspicious if an adult caught all of us children with watches. They were too expensive for children to own."

He continued, "Oh, also, we will be arriving in March, so the weather is very unpredictable. Wear or carry your coat at all times. You will blend in better."

"Yes sir, I will," Cully answered giving a mock American salute. Lian thought it funny, and saluted back the same way.

The group of six climbed a few steps, moved toward a short door in the wall, to stooping slightly to go through. When they emerged into a shallow cave, Hans closed the door and arranged the huge bushes that stood in front of the cave opening until it was completely covered.

# Chapter XIII

**O**ddly, I noticed that the little cave we emerged from brought me into what felt like an electrical atmosphere. I was being pushed forward as my feet and hands began tingling. A feeling that spread a mild charge throughout my body. As I passed through this "curtain", I became aware of a heightened sense of self-awareness. The electrical effects faded away. I looked forward. My first utterance was, "I…, oh my…. My head hurts." I supported my head in my left hand.

"It will pass quickly, Cully. We don't feel it as strongly as you do."

As I looked up, I saw we were standing in a forest from which we could view at a distance, rows of beautiful, classic early 20th century buildings. I turned back and gasped an intake of air, placing my hand on my chest. Before me, stood five children.

I asked, "Which one is which?"

Hans replied, "I am the tallest of all the children with boring, brown hair," as he grabbed my hand to shake it formally.

"How do you do, Hans?" I, bowing a bit, replied.

Ada came up to me next, "I am the dark-haired one with the straight bangs." She shook my hand.

Next, Klaus approached me, "I am the smallest, but I am strong. I am with blond hair, as you can see."

I shook his hand.

Lian stepped up like a soldier, "I am the smartest, but you can tell me by my blond hair and blue eyes." I shook his hand and noticed he had beautiful, crystal blue eyes.

Finally, Clotilda walked to me, "I am with long, brown hair I always keep in the same ribbon, and brown eyes." I shook her hand. Then I reviewed each child to myself by what they told me; first, there was tall Hans, then bob-cut Ada, blond Klaus, blue-eyed Lian, and long-haired Clotilda.

"I think I can remember each and every one of you. Where do we go first? Oh, and do I suddenly detect a serious German accent in all of you or am I imagining it?"

Lian just shrugged, "We are home, and it is Germany, so we are speaking German." I nodded my head once, missing the implication at that time.

The tall Hans pointed to a building off in the distance. "That house is unoccupied. The owner is gone for a few months, she told......," He stopped himself. The others looked at him warily.

"Anyway, it is empty for now. We know where the key is, and the neighbors on either side are not there. They are Jewish. Rich ones, but that doesn't matter. A Nazi colonel and his men took most of their furnishings, but left Frau Heinrich's house alone because she is a German nationalist, and hangs a Nazi flag on her second story. You can see it from here."

I squinted and looked, "I see it. You want me there?"

Klaus said, "They will not bother you with the flag hanging. They already searched the neighborhood, and know the lady who lives there. But they don't know she has any relatives. You are a niece from her dead brother that is staying in the house while she is gone. Also, a few of the other houses on the block are occupied with other rich, non-Jews."

"Very clever, Klaus."

I ruffled his hair, then stopped as he smiled. "Oh, I'm sorry. You are a cute kid."

Klaus gave a big grin, "I am a kid in most senses here. You can ruffle my hair anytime you want."

I laughed, and then shook the shoulder of each child. "Here we go."

The group emerged from the cluster of bushes which was part of a larger park and walked toward a house. I noticed that three of the kids lagged back, and two walked with me. I did not question it. Soon we arrived at the building. It was at 124 MarienstraBe. Fortunately, no one was around on the block, so we walked up many stairs to a landing, crowding onto it before attacking more stairs in another direction. It was a tall, skinny house to me squished between two other skinny houses. Hans got a key from his pocket.

We entered the house quietly being wary.

Ada said, "Stay here."

Although, no one seemed to be there, the children split up and ran all over the house to make sure no one was occupying the house anyway, and they joined me back in the foyer.

The foyer was magnificent. I was in awe as I gazed around. Despite it looking old-fashioned to me, I loved the ornate lampshades that adorned the table lights. Wallpaper hung everywhere. I walked into a living room to my left passing a tall staircase in front of me. I was astonished how beautifully the rest of the house was decorated. It was lush with damask drapes and furniture. It had beautiful Indian carpets, exquisite portrait and landscape paintings hanging large on the walls. The furniture stood solid, as if it had never been sat on. It was the formal parlor of the house where guests were received. Ada motioned for me to follow her through a swinging door to which the kitchen appeared. It was the largest kitchen I had ever been in. It looked like a kitchen for an old restaurant with counters everywhere, an island of smooth wood bare at its disuse. Pans and pots hung from a frame above the huge island in the center of the room. The room was spotless. Following Ada through and around the kitchen, and exited another door into the formal dining room. I had been speechless since viewing the first room, and my awe only grew. The table was a beautiful wood with scalloped edges and chairs that matched. The seats were also clothed in the most beautiful rose material. The windows were tall as in the parlor and covered with sheer curtains draped on either side by exquisite deep purple and gold fabric drapes. I think they were the tallest curtained windows I had ever seen.

Clotilda approached me and said, "Ok, look in amazement, but wait till you see the rest of the upstairs."

"Whose house is this? Are you sure we won't get caught being here?" I asked pensively.

Clotilda sighed and reported to me that the house was that of Frau Heinrich, a widow, and that she was traveling the South American continent after her husband died. She told me that Frau Heinrich would not be returning for quite a while, maybe three months or more depending on the war. There had been some bombing by the Allies the previous year, but not since. This was March 1942. Hans told me that the constant cloud cover at this time of year prevented the British nor the Allies from successful bombing raids. The bombs kept missing the factories, of which there were many. Still, we had only a month before circumstances could endanger our situation.

One more challenge from me, "C'mon, how can you know all that?"

"We're children," Klaus added, "We watched her leave with luggage when we were looking for a place you could stay. We asked the neighbors by telling them that Frau Heinrich let us come by for hot chocolate once in a while. We went down the block on the other side of the neighbors that had been removed to confirm this. They each confirmed the same thing. That's before we came and got you. We had to plan a lot of things before we went to get you."

"But you are just children. How would you know to do all of this?" I asked puzzled.

"We are all very smart. And remember, we've been here in this situation before. Also, we became adults when we entered your world and decided together the things that had to be covered for your arrival. We didn't want to leave anything to chance," Klaus continued, "You must realize that this will never work if we didn't know what we were doing and what you must do!" Klaus' impatience with me was beginning.

I stood in the dining room looking at all five of them impressed with such maturity, but having the most adorable faces of children. This truly was the strangest feeling; however, I decided to abandon dwelling on it. I wanted to do whatever it took to help their steadfast ambition. I always loved history. My favorite focus was, as a matter of fact, always on World War II. I had read Elie Wiesel's *Night*, Marcus Zusak's *The Book Thief*, John Boyne's *The Boy in the Striped Pajamas*, Anne Frank's *Diary of a Young Girl*, Jane Yolen's *The Devil's Arithmetic*, and Wendy Lower's *Hitler's Furies*, and so many other books.

Clotilda brushed my arm, "We need to go up and see your bedroom."

I climbed multiple stairs, again, with all five of the children and entered what looked like a small bedroom lavishly decorated for children with twin beds. There were two more rooms to match. Clotilda pushed me along, and I peeked into the largest bedroom with a huge bed also exquisitely decorated. The room was spacious with a small desk by a huge window, two richly dark red, wing-backed chairs with a small table in between, near the fireplace, and the most comfortable looking velvet window seat. I loved window seats. It had thick cushions and pillows on it like a couch. The window was tall and wide enough to accommodate an adult who may have wanted to nap on it.

Finally, Ada took my hand and led me to a wardrobe. She opened it to era-appropriate civilian clothing.

"You can wear any of this, I think. When you're here or not working that is. Frau Heinrich was not thin, but you can try them on and see if these things fit. You are more proportioned. Although, if they don't fit, we'll have to adjust them where we can."

I was so amazed at the quality of the clothing. So, I immediately grabbed a wrap dress in dark blue with large pink blooms, and an average pair of black, low heels, and tried the dress on. I was relieved. It fit well-enough. So did the plain shoes. I turned to Ada and asked her if there were any other shoes to wear.

"Yes, but you do not want to stand out. We need you to be average. And, I would change that dress for the grey suit there," she said and she pointed into the armoire

"Of course," I replied.

"It will be warmer and match others who wear wool suits right now."

After we established that I had enough civilian clothing to rotate weekly for a month, we raided the kitchen. There were a few cans, a few boxes, the cold box was empty, but Hans told me that an iceman came around with a truck. I needed instruction on where the ice went. I was not going to have any gourmet meals since I was used to a modern kitchen, and my husband enjoyed cooking the most. It became obvious. The children spent a little time with me educating me on what the average breakfast, lunch, and dinner was, and how to shop at the local market. It was actually enticing to shop for food in a market where much of the food was out of stalls. There was some rationing, but nothing too stressful yet because they assured me that in this particular neighborhood, after the Jews were removed, there were still quite a few well-to-do residents. So, there would be a market close by. They further told me that one of them would always go with me to the market.

Suddenly, the doorbell chimed. I froze. Ada went down to the door like she owned the house. When she opened the door, Lian was pushing me up the back stairs in the kitchen to the second floor. He grabbed my arm and put me in another bedroom. I had no time to admire the furnishings as anxiety crawled up my neck. I overheard Ada tell the gentleman that they were cousins of Frau Heinrich, and her niece was upstairs napping. She must have been convincing because I heard the door close and Ada ran up the stairs.

Lian said, "It was the local German Police patrol, but everyone knows they are Gestapo thugs."

I asked how he knew that. Ada replied that on the next block were two wealthy Jewish families, and the police took them away. Some officer high up showed up and ransacked the house taking all the valuables away in a truck.

Klaus answered, "When are you going to understand that we are children. We roamed everywhere unnoticed to check out this neighborhood for your stay. All the Jews here, and there were only a few in this area, have been removed and their valuables confiscated. But the non-Jewish people here were pretty much respected and left alone. As long as we display the Nazi flag over the balcony, they will leave us alone! That man was just checking the security of the neighborhood. He was, actually, glad that someone was occupying the house."

I paused for a minute, then asked Klaus quietly, "Okay, so what you are basically saying is 'stop asking questions about how you know something'. Am I right?"

All five heads nodded up and down, except Ada elbowed Klaus in the side and ordered, "You will be patient with her!" Klaus raised his hands in defense, nodding vigorously. I think I figured out who was in charge.

"So, where do we start first?" I prompted.

"With a reconnaissance mission," said Hans.

However, Ada chaperoned me first to the market, and we strolled to purchase a few edibles, mostly bread and cheese. We took them back, ate some accompanied by soup. Then I walked with Ada, Lian, Hans, and Clotilda to the back of the railroad yard building in Stuttgart. It was a long walk to me, but then I came from a mobile society. The children pointed out the tall, wide, brick 'roundhouse' they called it, alongside the back of the building. and I could see the windows at the top that went all the way around. What I saw behind it and to the side was a long, ordinary brick building with a depot platform that extended well out of my sight. We saw no one except, I think, two military security guards, at this particular time, off in the distance. It was 7:00 p.m., and Hans and the group wanted to show me Mina's hideout.

"No," said Ada, "not now. She could be in there. We don't want her to see Cully yet. A better time would be in the morning after she goes to school."

"How stupid," said Hans, "I did not think. I don't know what time it is."

I told him that it was 7:05. He shook his head, "I liked having a watch. Oh well."

The children and I walked back toward our neighborhood being careful not to draw attention to ourselves. There were a few people walking, but no one paid much attention to a me walking with two children. The other two of the children walked way ahead and were talking to each other. I could tell that the neighborhood was rather upscale, but I also noticed that people did seem generally to look at other people, but with furtive glances. I walked casually with a child on either side of me and strolled up to the house that we occupied. We purposefully climbed all the stairs. Before I could ring the bell, Lian pushed my arm down and the door opened with Klaus standing in the foyer. I was prodded inside by Lian; the others followed, and Hans closed the door.

"You have to pretend you belong here," said Hans, "You don't go ringing the bell."

"Oh, sorry," I cringed.

# Chapter XIV

**T**he next morning as I descended the steep stairs, I overheard what sounded like an argument.

"We need to take her to where she can see Mina, Mina's mother, and where Mina is hiding D'avia," Klaus added.

"I think we need to get her the job first," said Ada.

"We can't. She will be expected to start work immediately, and we can't afford that until she has met the girls involved in her goal!" said Clotilda

Lian seconded the motion. He looked at Ada and then pointed to Clotilda. Klaus, and Hans who all had their right hands up.

"Alright, another reconnaissance mission first," said Ada exasperated.

It was a little warmer when the group entered the forest this day. I was satisfied that it wasn't so far from the house that we were occupying that it would take an hour to get there. Klaus said that it was maybe two kilometers we had to walk. I had asked if there was any transportation like a taxi or something. Hans looked shocked at me.

"Most everybody walks here. Many vehicles were commandeered for the military. There are trams but they run locally. We may be able to get bicycles later when we leave with the girls, but, for now, we walk."

I found this to be true because I saw several people on the sidewalks moving here and there. I had never had to walk very far where I came from because my job was strategically placed not too far from Union Station. I did not work out because I was always tired when I came home. And, in the morning, I was always rushing to get my train. I only hoped that I was up to this new adventure of walking everywhere. I also hoped I would make few blunders getting used to the different time period. I was beginning to feel the danger.

Hans suddenly barred me with his arm at a street corner. He asked, "Where are your papers we gave you?"

"In my purse," I told him.

"OK, good."

"Don't scare me like that!" I retorted.

"You need to understand that if the police stop us, you must always have your papers on you. Leaving them at home is suspicious, and they will take action, and you will get attention. We can't have that. Being obscure is our goal."

"I know, Hans, I'll try not to get upset with you, but don't ever startle me like that. I nearly jumped out of my skin!" I snapped at him.

Lian and the others started to giggle at Hans and me. In fact, Clotilda had a hard time stopping her giggling until Hans gave her a soft whap on the back.

"Ow, that hurt," Clotilda said rubbing her back.

"Clotilda, it would be suspicious if people saw us laughing too much also. Remember, we need to be invisible, more or less," Hans barked at her.

However, people on the road did glance our way because I was laughing with five children. Three kids followed behind me, and two of the children held my hands as we moved on.

Abruptly, a car came racing down the street honking its horn to get people out of its way. It was a long open car with soldiers. Despite its speed it came to a skidding halt next to a couple and their children on the other side of the road. They were carrying luggage, apparently not a good sign, because one of the officers jumped out and demanded to see their papers. Lian told me to keep moving and don't look at them. But I sneaked a peek as I kept walking. The officer began hitting the man with his crop, and told two soldiers to get out of the car and walk the people back the way we were headed to the train station. I could hear all of this because the officer was yelling so loud, everybody in the area could hear him. The other pedestrians turned to stare or turned away and kept walking.

When the six of us arrived at one of the crossroads of the train, we veered down the train tracks and into a gulley below next to a forest. After a few steps, the children entered the forest and I, looking around, followed them. I felt like I had walked 10 miles instead of a little over one mile. Although I had oxford shoes on, my feet hurt. I had a passing thought. *Because I was used to wearing heels, my feet conformed to them more comfortably.* After walking through the trees for 15 minutes, Lian grabbed me pushing me down on the ground. All the children hit the ground immediately. They had heard a crack of a branch some distance ahead and didn't want to take any chances. As the person slowly came into view, Hans whispered, "It's Mina!"

"She must not see us!" Ada hissed.

I had learned not to ask why, but just go along with them. We stayed still for a few minutes when Mina turned around and went back the way she had come. As she disappeared further away, the children began rising and helped me to my feet. I brushed off my coat and legs, and said to all, "She is a beautiful child if a little gaunt."

"As we all are," said Ada who spied me with a quirky half-smile.

I smirked at her and said, "Of course you are. I just mentioned it because she looks like an angel being so white blond as she is."

Lian added, "She is an angel; trust me."

Our group continued to walk in the direction from which Mina had come, however our steps were taken with more stealth. After five minutes more of walking, the children stopped me and took me to the left near an outcropping of the forest floor. This took another two minutes to walk, but we soon arrived well back and into the trees. Hans quietly pointed out the 'roundhouse' in the distance using binoculars. I could see where Mina's father worked, and where her family lived below on the first and second floor. I nodded, began to move back when Hans grabbed my arm and indicated for me to wait. Lying down on the forest floor once again, he whispered for me to watch the house. It took thirty minutes of waiting. I had laid my head down. Then Hans tapped me on the shoulder and handed me the binoculars. I looked up and saw a blond woman, skinny, in a weathered dark dress, short socks with oxford shoes on. She was pinning up her laundry behind the station house about three hundred yards from the edge of the forest, I guessed. Actually, I'm really bad at guessing distances.

The children crept along the approximate distance of one hundred yards opposite from the tree line, and I followed keeping as low to the ground as possible. I knew I would mess up my clothes, but I thought that was not significant to worry about. My focus on the woman became hypnotizing. I never took my eyes away from her in case the woman looked up. Then, Hans gave a signal with his fist to stop. Everyone laid still. I could make out bruises on the woman's left arm. I also saw that she had a fading black eye. The wheels in my head began turning figuring out why Mina was abused. I

73

had seen movies where the father abused the mother, the mother abused her little child, and the little child abused a favorite stuffed animal or a doll. Trickle-down effect. I hung my head for a minute trying to hold back my emotion when Ada tapped my shoulder.

"Don't cry! Or you are of no use to us. You must be strong. Fight those tears. You can cry later, much later!"

I nodded my head cooperating with her and held back the tears by changing my mood to one of anger. We crawled a little further, and, by this time, I was getting filthy, but I didn't care. I followed those children until they stopped me again just this side of a large, fallen log. On the other side was a bunch of leaves, as if someone raked them into a pile, with quite a lot of forest detritus which would challenge anyone coming into the woods from that angle. The trees also kept the forest deep in shadow even though it was a bright day, right up to the glare of the sun beyond the trees. The hovel was not apparent from what I expected for Mina's hiding place. Then, Hans tapped me again and whispered that I was to start turning around as quietly as I possible could to crawl back where we came from. I nodded my head and dove too quickly right into a partially standing stick that pierced my side before I could stop it. I spoke, "Ow!" and, turning me over, Hans' hand clapped over my mouth. His look darted to the roundhouse. The woman had gone inside. We waited for about five minutes. There was no movement from the ground around Mina's secret burrow or the house. Hans looked at my side. The stick had driven into my side through my dress. It must have been very sharp. A burning pain spread through my side.

The children crawled around me, and covered my mouth with two or three hands. I felt suffocated until Hans drew out the stick as quickly as possible. A muffled scream escaped my lips. Tears started streaming down my face. I couldn't help it as I looked at Ada. She whispered, "I wasn't talking about those kinds of tears, dear." Again, I barely nodded my head while the hands remained on my mouth. Hans crawled up to my face and whispered to me, "I don't think it hit any important places. I have stopped the bleeding with part of my shirt. Clotilda worked her scarf around your middle. We still had to crawl a little way. Can you make it?"

I nodded my head again, and the hands on my mouth retreated. However, my chin shook, I didn't open my mouth for fear of hollering. Ada gave me her scarf, and I tied it around my mouth in case I needed to push any pain back that came humming out of my mouth. On my forearms, pushing with my shoes, I crawled behind them. When we got back to the railroad tracks, Lian became our lookout, and we had already risen to walk, so we climbed up to the tracks, and I followed them back to the crossroads. Before approaching, though, we made sure to brush off any leaves on our clothes so we wouldn't stand out among the people on the sidewalks. As I held my arm close to my side, I tried to keep a calm face even though my teeth were locked in a tight clench. I pulled the scarf further over my forehead. I tried not to grab my side; Hans tightened the patch job, and we walked less than two kilometers back to the house. All I could think about was getting back to the house. It seemed like it took an hour because we had to walk unobtrusively. Then Lian told me it would only take 15 minutes to get there.

# Chapter XV

As soon as I got into the house and the heavy door was securely shut, I leaned against the banister and let out a low, long moan. Klaus ran to find a first-aid kit. Clotilda helped me lie down on the couch, and Hans began pulling my blouse up to examine the damage.

"You know this feels a little weird with a child looking up my blouse," I moaned.

Hans grinned. He said, "Think of me as a small doctor." He made me laugh even though my side hurt like hell.

After Klaus brought some bandages and whiskey to the couch, I said, "I don't drink whiskey," to which he replied, "No, but you'll crave it to get rid of the pain and get that wound disinfected." Klaus also brought tweezers, so Hans could pick out any remaining pieces of wood from my wound. Being that I was in excruciating pain, I grabbed the bottle of whiskey from Klaus and took two big gulps, which made me cough and then yell, "Ow" between the coughs. I sipped some more whiskey after that which helped the pain ease ever so slightly.

"Okay, now rest, Cully. I have cleaned the wound and picked out only two little wood pieces. I've packed it with bandages for now. But you need you to drink more whiskey because Ada is going sew it closed. You understand?"

I looked at Hans somewhat bleary-eyed, and said, "Ochhh…kaaa."

"She's almost there," said Clotilda.

The rest of the kids couldn't help snickering in response to Clotilda's statement.

"Okay, we have to be serious now; we have to close this wound or it could get infected. It will mess up our plans because it will put Cully in danger," Hans face was strained as he stared fixedly at the group.

The children calmed down from their noise making and went off to the kitchen to find something to eat. Only Ada stayed with me holding my hand. "You will heal. You have to. This is so important," she whispered, as close to my ear as possible, "You are important."

I couldn't really respond since I was relaxing nicely into a stupor courtesy of the whiskey. When Hans, Clotilda, Klaus, and Lian returned from the kitchen with some soup, I was oblivious to most of my surroundings. I just wanted to cuddle up and go to sleep, but Hans would have none of it. He gently shook my shoulder to make me alert and encouraged me to sip a little more whiskey while Ada was preparing the sewing needle with thread that she had found in a sewing basket on the living room floor.

After Ada carefully and slowly sewed up the wound, I asked her to hurry up and finish, so I could sleep. The soup went untouched. "I'm already done, Cully. Take a nap now while we plan our next move." I mumbled something back to her, and then the world outside of my head disappeared.

After what seemed minutes, I began to arouse my body from a stiff position. I turned over on the couch and all the kids were sitting on the floor looking at me.

"What?" I asked. "What's wrong?"

"Nothing," said Lian, "We were just trying to stare you awake. It's been three hours."

"It's okay," Ada said, "It's late, and we cannot do anything tonight, but we have to get you ready for tomorrow."

"What's tomorrow?" I asked.

"Your job starting," replied Clotilda.

"My what?" I swung my head from one to the other.

"Your first day of work," said Klaus, "You have to show up for this job in order to get travel papers. They are enormously important to our journey and rescue of the girls."

I sat up, a little too abruptly, my hand went to my head, while I accepted a cup of coffee from Clotilda. As I sipped, nothing tasted so good as hot coffee, I drank it all in silence, and then addressed the crew.

"Alright, where do I go to work? You've done everything else by supernatural means."

"You have to do this part by yourself. We won't be far away, but we can't be with you," said "Yes," I stuttered a little, "that will be a little daunting."

Hans added, "We know typists to the central Gestapo office are always needed because many German women are encouraged to stay home, but many serve the military in whatever function they can or at what they are useful. You will present yourself in a suitable uniform to those military personnel here in Stuttgart. Your fervor for nationalism needs to be in your demeanor when you present yourself at the Stuttgart headquarters."

"OK, now I'm scared."

"You will need every nerve you have," said Hans, "We need you to be calm, and act a little demur. Typists to administrative officers earn special privileges like travel papers, and the typists are always around staff officers. So, listen! Around the officers you need to be present, but invisible. Your listening skills need to be sharp, but unassuming."

"Also," added Klaus, "We will give you a map of general Stuttgart streets in the area. You must study it very carefully, so you know where to catch a bus for the city central. You are a widow. Working for the regime's Stuttgart office with your excellent administrative skills will make you valuable.

I thought a moment, and reflected to the children, "I'm actually pretty good with maps. I had to memorize downtown Chicago streets years ago. I'm a quick study. I think I can do that fairly well. It's being in the room with the officers that will make me nervous. I thought you said 'the SS'?"

"Yes, it stands for 'Shutzstaffel' or the Protection Squad. They are assigned to carry out any security issues without need for paying attention to higher military rank or without impunity."

"I have a suggestion," said Hans, "keep your mouth shut. The protocol is normally that you don't open your mouth unless you are asked a question in this office. Keep busy. The Nazi hierarchy is very strict about that all the way down to a mere colonel in a general staff position. You will be a civilian as a Gestapo employee. The Gestapo is a subdivision of the SS. One of its offices is dedicated to the policing and control of movement or travel of German citizens in the area to make sure they embrace the Nazi protocol and are not active participants in any secrecy involving the Jewish problem."

"Oh." I paused. "So where do I get the transfer?"

Ignoring my question, Hans continued, "You will show up at the reception desk at general staff headquarters on Snauffen Street and tell them that you have been sent to work as a typist in the Security Control office of a Colonel Berchtold. They always need good typists. The use typewriters, but also code machines to send messages. He will be most grateful to have an accomplished typist."

"When you arrive, it is very hectic at the headquarters, so you will ask the receptionist where the typing pool is located. He or she will probably be on the phone. They'll give you a clipboard register to sign in, give you a pass to the floor where you actually present yourself for work." Hans stopped to take a breath and continued, "There are only a few staff officers. However, there is a desk of a Junior Private, who will instruct you to the proper office."

Hans further commented, "We know you are scared, so think of it as acting, like on a stage; think Shakespeare. You become that person. Don't try to think about Cully Rollins; you are 'Eves Obermardt', a well-dressed woman, intelligent, but reserved, mildly assertive, but with an air of enthusiasm." Then he walked into the kitchen.

"I understand," I said, "but it is a little daunting. I am Eves Obermardt. I don't particularly smile. I report with a determination to do my job. I respect the officers while demonstrating a purpose to be of value to the command. However, I must also be low-key and willing to demonstrate any skills they will value."

Klaus stood up from the couch, "That is very good, Cully. I think you will be fine. Most excellent. Remember, you must mention that you are a widow of an SS soldier from the East. That must be your storyline, so that they will accept you without suspicion. He is Colonel Berchtold, but that is all the information you have to give. Okay?"

"Yes, I can do this." I stood up straight, shoulders back, and assumed the position of a serious German worker. I wanted to feel who I would be. The children focused their eyes on me with tears welling up. I gazed down at them and asked, "What?"

Lian spoke first, "We are so proud of you, Cully. You have no idea how important you are to this mission."

I relaxed, "Why am I so important to 'this mission' instead of anybody else?"

"It will reveal itself to you when we achieve it. It is our last chance," Ada whispered.

"All this secrecy, and I know I'm here to save those girls, but why are they so important to save? I feel out of the loop on information here."

Hans had returned, standing behind me, "Okay, I will tell you something. But this is all I can tell you. One of the girls is going to become very important in history if she is able to grow up. I cannot tell you which one because I don't know. However, I am sure about one of them being critical to the future, and not letting either die because we don't know which one. Although, we don't want either to die, but it is significant that both survive. And, we know that you are the only one that can help us. I, honestly, don't know the answer to that either, but I know."

I looked at Hans soberly, "I understand. You gave me your last name."

"It is a good German name, that's all."

Everyone climbed the stairs and prepared for bed. Ada showed me the clothes in the wardrobe that I would wear the next day. It was not exactly stylish, but of heavy quality wool. She promised to help me with my hair in the morning. We all said 'good-night', and I climbed into a very soft, though not firm, bed and fell immediately to sleep. The next thing I knew, it was morning. I dressed. Ada came in to fix my hair, as promised, and I put on an oh, so attractive hat. *Yuck.* One thing remained. I still had remnants of lipstick on my mouth. I took some cream from the bureau and wiped it off to neatly replace it.

"That was good to notice," said Ada. "Lipstick is generally worn on civilian personnel. Although, the regime emphasized natural beauty."

"Anything else?" I looked in the mirror on the wardrobe. I almost laughed; I looked like a whole other person. All I could say was a quiet, "Wow."

I had an old-fashioned hairstyle, a cocked hat of the time, a lovely dark-gray skirt and jacket, an off-white blouse, mid heels, and a small shoulder-strap handbag.

Ada examined my look. She nodded her head in approval. "You look perfect!"

"Okay, I just have to think 'Eves Obermardt'. I've already had most of the streets memorized, and I have a good sense of direction, so here I go."

Ada's eyebrows went up pondering my look with a mix of admiration and, what looked like hope.

I said apprehensively, "Are you sure I'm ready, Ada?"

"Well, all we can do is try, Cully. I know you are a very intelligent person, more than you give yourself credit for. We just have to try," Ada sighed.

Ada and I took the stairs down to the living room where Klaus, Hans, Lian, and Clotilda were waiting for me. Their eyes went wide with approval. Hans gave me the directions to the administration building for the Gestapo in Stuttgart near the city center, and told me he and Lian would walk me to the tram. Then he and Lian would go their own way carrying two books as if walking to school, but in reality, hiking to the city center, and put themselves in a niche not too far from the headquarters building. They could not assist me anymore. Lian reminded me that when I speak it will come out as German, and when spoken to, I will hear it in English. His only warning was for me not to use any American idioms or expressions, but stay with straight, clear sentences, and address everyone as 'Herr' or 'Frau' or 'Fraülein' and their last name if I knew it. Most officers would introduce themselves to me, so that I could address them by name. The uniforms themselves didn't carry their names.

Hans asked one last question I wasn't prepared for, "Eves, what are our names and ages if you are ever stopped and asked, "I stood stock still, turned to clever Hans, and reported, "Hans, Ada, Klaus, Lian, and Clotilda. And I will make it easy for myself going with; they are all 10 years old."

"And what if someone makes a comment that that is a little unnatural?" Clotilda asked.

"I'll tell anyone who asks that I have five children.

The children looked at me concentrating. Then Hans said, "That's preposterous. But, let's hope no one asks for now."

I hugged all the children together, straightened my suit and set off with Hans and Lian trailing me down the front steps and to the right on the sidewalk with eyes direct toward my 'mission' as I thought of it. *Let the adventure begin.*

# Chapter XVI

**As** I rounded the corner approaching the headquarters, soldiers in groups looked at me. I suppose in their era, that I was considered beautiful without my make-up. The crowds became thicker as I realized any stores that were open were not far from the building. Other soldiers passing didn't ignore me either. I walked casually trying not to draw too much attention to myself, and was gratified when I saw other German women strolling with each other and sometimes with baby buggies.

Once in the front door, I spotted the secretary at a high desk at the base of the wide stairs ascending and, alternately, descending. As a matter of fact, she was on the phone as Hans had told me. She waved her hand at me, balanced the phone on her shoulder, and put a registration book or log on top of the counter. I read some of the names and tried to copy their left-leaning writing style, so as not to make mine stand out. I felt panic rise in my throat when a soldier approached and asked me if he could help me.

"Fraülein, where do you want to go?"

I took a deep breath, and said, "I need to report for a typing job like I had before the war broke out. I lost my job because my employer was Jewish."

"Oh," he said and pointed up the stairs, "Just take these stairs to the third floor, and there will be a Private there to help you," he offered.

"Thank you, sir," I said, trying to control my voice.

He looked at me a little odd, "It is my pleasure."

I stared into his eyes and said, "Thank you."

"You already said that," he said with a beautiful, half-smile. All I could think of was to bow my head a little and begin climbing the stairs. However, as I climbed, a small, ashamed thought peeked its way through to my conscience mind, *damn, he's beautiful.*

As I climbed the stairs and arrived at the third floor, there was the Private immediately to my left that called me over and asked what my business was. He pushed his glasses up and surveyed me up and down my person.

I replied, "Eves Oberhardt reporting."

He asked, "State your business."

I thought quickly, as my eyes scanned the wall behind him, "I am here to work in a typing position." I held my breath.

"Very good. You will report to Room 334 down the hall, knock, wait for an invitation to enter, and then do so," he replied.

I quickly walked away, turned the corner, and plastered myself against the wall of an extremely small anteroom. I talked in my head, and pleaded with me to calm down and control my breathing. *I had never been so scared in my life. Terrified would better describe it, I thought.* But I whispered to myself out loud, "Self, get it under control. Remember, you are a loyal citizen of Hitler's Germany, named Eves Oberhardt. You express a pleasant, quiet attractiveness, yet with an earnestness to do a job. Hold your head up, and look straight." With that self-instruction, I rolled around the wall on my shoulder to no one in the hall. *Thank God for small favors, I thought.*

Within a few steps, I approached the door that read '334' and knocked. There was no answer. I remained patient. Startling me, a man pulled open the door swiftly.

I jumped back and remarked, "Oh! I said and waited for a reaction."

"Sorry if I startled you, Fraülein. I was just leaving," said an older officer, about 50ish, and a little paunchy. He whisked by me. My eyes followed him, but then I heard myself being called for, so I abruptly turned toward the open door trying to calm my panicky heart and saw a female desk clerk looking at me. I approached her desk and addressed her respectfully according to the sign on her desk, informing me she was Fraülein Schmidt. She treated me more like a thing than a person. She didn't even look at me. Even so, I kept my demeanor the same and followed her instructions to take a seat at a desk surrounded by other busily typing women. She provided me with instruction that I had a full basket on my right. She told me to begin typing each paper on what was an 'antique' typewriter to me. *Typing on the big heavy typewriter would build muscles in my fingers,* I joked to myself. Within seconds, my fingers froze on the keys. I could not believe it-every document I read was in English. Therefore, I typed as strongly as I could. I had no idea that my fingers would need so much force. I prayed to myself that I was not noticed and doing all right.

I said nothing to the clerk, rose and delivered a few copies to her. One scan of the typed copies made her look up at me for the first time and said, "You will be useful. Now put the finished copies in the side basket at your desk. There will be no need for you to approach me again. Is that understood?" She rose to knock on another door set into the back of the office, entered and immediately came out closing the door. Within a few seconds she told me to go to the same door, knock lightly, and wait for permission to enter. I rose and did as I was told. As I opened the door, I saw many desks, lots of noise from phones, what looked to me like telex machines going, and some kind of machine spitting out paper. There was another door at the side I was pointed to. I knocked with tight nerves.

"Come in, come in" an officer said waving his hand for me to enter as the door opened. I was instructed to stand in front of his desk. He had as huge mop of hair, bushy eyebrows, and a very large mustache that I found repellent. I walked over, carefully, feeling like I was walking on a minefield. There I stood for what seemed like an hour in front of his desk, although, in reality, it was only a few minutes. He had been perusing my typed copies and some paper on his desk looking back and forth to my copies. He said, "You are a most exceptional typist, Fraülein."

"Thank you, but it is Frau," I replied as calmly as I could muster.

He did not acknowledge my statement.

"I have an officer who generates security papers for travel. He could use an excellent typist temporarily. Unlike you, he currently has a rather incompetent dunderhead. Have a seat for a moment," he instructed.

Once he was on the phone jabbering away in German, a wave of giddiness washed over me. I understood every word of his rapid-fire German. I tried to keep a straight face, but it was a challenge, and I only let a small smile arise as the officer hung up the phone and told me to leave his office and turn left going all the way to the end of the hall to see a Colonel Berchtold. As I left his office, closing the door, I turned left to see that in front of me was a long hall, but as I traversed the aisles of desks, personnel, and noise I had been in, I walked into the open-doored room of Colonel Berchtold's office and was struck dumb. He was the man that had helped me with directions on the main floor. I edged in and stood in front of his desk while he was finishing writing something, then stamping it, then blowing on it, and finally tossing it into a wooden tray on the corner of his desk. Momentarily, he looked up and seemed surprised as well.

"Well, well, Fraülein, so you end up seeing me as it turns out. Gutner, go see Captain Muetger. I need to use this young woman to do something for me," he said abruptly, "And close the door behind you." The soldier left promptly.

"Please have a seat, Fraulein," he gestured with his hand.

I moved to the chair and remembered not to cross my legs, but to sit up straight in a lady-like posture, legs tilted to the right. He folded his hands in front of his eyes as he seemed to stare across the room. Soon he put them down and addressed me, "Fraulein, are you able to work long hours? Do you have children at home? What is your situation? Oh, and what is your name for my records?"

"I am a widow, Herr Berchtold, so it's 'Frau Eves Obermardt' and I have seven children. But the oldest is able to care for the others while I am at work." The man I was facing was disarmingly attractive. I had to focus on his nose, so I could concentrate.

"Alright, Frau Obermardt, I can use you. I may catch up faster with my workload. My current aide is like a child. I have to tell him not only what to do, but how to do it in most cases," he shrugged. "We will get started immediately, if you don't mind."

"Of course, I don't."

Herr Berchtold directed me to a desk not too far from his that faced his at a right angle. He picked up a pack of papers and deposited them in front of me on my new desk.

"These are travel papers, memoranda, and letters that have to be typed up. As you finish each one, just place it in that basket on my desk and I will approve their accuracy. The majority of them are vital for military personnel and some civilians and, of course, for Jew exportation. I do have to make sure each is appropriately correct before it is signed. Then I will tell you how to summon someone for delivery of them. Oh, and everyone must carry security papers for identification whether leaving Stuttgart or entering. Some have to carry papers to Central Office inside Stuttgart depending on their purpose and, of course, ethnic orientation. I understand your former employer was a Jew?" he asked.

"That is correct," I answered warily.

"I assume he was removed and the business closed?"

"That is correct," I answered again.

"You may relax, Frau Obermardt. It was not your responsibility to secure him, his family, nor his business," he said cordially. "And, I am glad to have such an excellent typist assigned to me. I think this will provide me less frustration and help me to get closer to approving security papers and dealing with traveling issues more promptly. The military's basic personnel know to put them in enough ahead of time to get them reviewed. "I will leave you alone right now unless you have any questions," his eyebrows raised.

"I think I have what I need. The forms here, the applications here, and the letters and memorandum in that basket," I pointed to as I eyed him directly unsmiling.

"That is correct. Someone who knows how to do things," he muttered as he walked out the door.

I began assembling the papers for my first assignment and started doing the work. I was surprised to find the work actually very basic and not at all challenging. But, then, I thought, *I was an executive assistant for years. Duhhhh.* I could easily handle this work while working with my accomplices to plan our rescue of the two girls. I felt more confident as the day went on.

After leaving work, I walked home, but not alone. I suspected my stalkers were Hans and Lian, but did not certify this until I turned on them near the house. "Gotcha," I said. They both smiled and encouraged me to get inside. As soon as I did, they all hugged me and wanted to know how my day had gone. They sat on the parlor couch by my chair, and I explained to them what happened in as much detail as I could. Ada had prepared a meal, and we moved to the dining room where we ate hungrily. Klaus had been snooping around and showed us that he found some more money hidden in cans around the house and on top of the wardrobe. We had enough money for food. After dinner, the children spread a map of Stuttgart out on the table, and we began to plan how many visits to make and observe Mina and her family, when to spot Mina going to her hiding place, and to work out a timetable for grabbing the girls and leaving for Switzerland. I knew it would be a tough trip, but my heart was in the planning and helping these strange children to accomplish a goal I did believe in.

Hans said that we had to give it three weeks for me to work and become 'invisible', so to speak, in the office environment. Just another face is what I wanted to be. There were other women in a sort of 'typing pool' I would call it. It reminded me of the movie *Valkyrie*, So, I inferred I had a privilege working in an office for an officer. Actually, it would have been better if I had been in amongst other non-descript women in the 'pool', but, alas, that was not to be. I, certainly, could not ask to be demoted out of the officer's office.

After the children and I made some tentative plans, our first venture was to take place the next evening. Again, we would walk, cross the train tracks and make a reconnaissance of the forest area where Mina's shelter was. At the same time, I would guesstimate the distance from the roundhouse to the bunker itself to see how much time we would have to cover during our escape process, since Mina's mother would enter the woods up to her felled log boundary not too close to the hidden shelter. However, anyone entering or exiting the hiding place could be seen in the distance, at least during the day. The other matter was that I had to make contact with Mina to let her know what we were planning. Hans said he would take care of the initial contact, so I would not terrify the little girl by a woman suddenly approaching her.

# Chapter XVII

"**How's** your side?" Ada asked as we were crossing the train tracks the next day near dusk to once again size up the situation we were facing.

"It is much better. You are amazing, but then again, so is my 'little doctor'," I laughed. We walked and walked, and, somehow, it didn't seem as tiring as the last time, but I think it was because of us walking to the tram, hustling to work and back to the tram on time, and then walking back to the house. We arrived at the forest edge where we had to begin walking as quietly as we could deep into the heavy treed area. It took us quite a while to reach our last position, but, as we did, we saw Mina going into the woods looking back over her shoulder toward the roundhouse, I assume. She crawled into a pile of brush and disappeared from view. We followed surreptitiously, like creeping spiders. Hans held up his hand for us to stop. The five of us bunched up behind a tree.

"We have to contact her today," Clotilda said. "She just got here, and we have at least three hours before her mother will call her."

"Are you sure? Already?" I asked.

"Yes, Klaus looked at the paper timetable again, and the dates. If we wait too long, we won't have the advantage of the girls getting used to you and trusting you," answered Clotilda.

"She's right," Ada agreed.

"Hans, are you on board with this?" I asked.

"Absolutely. I thought we would have more time, but we don't. The earlier the girls meet you, the better," he whispered.

We waited and listened for a few minutes after which we bent lower and started a slow movement toward the bushes that Mina disappeared into. I focused on what I could see of the round house through the trees while the others led me closer to Mina's secret hideout. Before I knew it, we were very close. Once again, Hans put his hand up. He looked at the rest of us, and indicated we were to stay while he crept closer. He was going to throw a pebble down to Mina before he entered her hiding place, so he would not startle her. One child approaching a another would seem less seem less threatening as an adult like me. So, I watched crouched behind a tree with the others. It was only a few minutes when Hans peeked out of the bushes and beckoned us forward. *So, with trepidation like spies, I thought,* I continued forward as noiselessly as possible with the others around me. Strangely, I didn't hear them making any noise, however, it was probably because I was so focused on me not making noise. As we approached the bushes, I saw a small arm come out between the leaves. It belonged to Hans. He was motioning for me to take his hand. As I did so, he waved with his other hand to get on my knees and crawl. Thank goodness I had the sense to put pants on this time under my dress. The entrance was longer than I would have imagined for a little forest bunker. It had to be at least six feet long and angled down at a somewhat steep angle. Branches, leaves, and roots were all nicely tucked around the log to form a support for the ceiling of the tunnel.

As I emerged into the actual room of the hovel, it reminded me not unlike the inside of what a teepee would look like, except much sturdier with dirt walls a badger would create. I immediately saw the girls in the corner and sat on my heels, crossed my hands over my heart, and smiled. My 'children' pushed me further in, so they could come in, and I moved around the circle shape of the hideout in front of the two girls. They seemed very small in comparison to me beside them. The girls' eyes were staring at me like four headlights. I tried to ease their apprehension with a small smile. When everyone was inside, I noticed that the room was actually quite spacious. There were several blankets under the girls and others covering the entire floor space.

Hans introduced me, "Mina, D'avia, this is Eves Obermardt. She is here to help you. Mina, who was holding hands with D'avia, whispered, "Are you really going to help us?"

I looked at Mina with the softest looking face I could muster, "Darling, I am going to take you away from here for good, if that's what you want. It might be dangerous, but we all are going to try to rescue you and D'avia and get you across the border to Switzerland."

"Yes, please. But that means we have to go through the Black Forest. How are you going to manage that? Papa says no one returns from the Black Forest," she croaked.

I gazed at here trying to take them both in. Mina and D'avia did not have much weight on them. Mina more so than D'avia, but they didn't look ill, they looked emaciated with a dirt smudged on them everywhere. Mina was blond, with blue eyes, and a plain, but pretty face. She wore a whitish dress with a dark sweater that I could tell was well worn like it was the only thing she owned. D'avia had on similar clothing, but her dress was dark with a tiny print on it. She wore a gray sweater, and had bobbed, dark brown, thick hair. It was actually a warmer climate in the bunker due to a single lantern. D'avia appeared frightened of me, so I did not lean forward to touch her. I decided she had to grow to trust me. But then she had to do it quickly.

Hans continued, "Mina, Eves got a job, and she is going to get travel papers. It might take two or three more weeks because she has to establish herself at her job, but she does work for the Colonel of Security and Travel."

Mina turned to look at him and then her eyes went wide which I thought was odd.

Mina said, "Hans, you're really here! It is so good to see you Ada, Klaus, Lian, and Clotilda."

"We all missed you." Hans said with affection. At that moment Ada, Klaus, Lian, and Clotilda all smiled at her without making a sound. I expected the children to start chattering all at once, but they didn't. Then, I remembered: sound could funnel up through the tunnel. Silence was a necessity. Mina moved closer to me on her knees and touched my cheek with her hand. Her dirty hand approached my cheek, but I didn't mind. Slowly, tears began welling up in her eyes, and D'avia joined her touching my other cheek with her dirty hand. I stayed stock still so as not to frighten the girls and just kept smiling. Mina whispered, "You truly are here. You're real and not a dream."

I answered quietly, "I am truly here and not a dream."

D'avia broke in, "Mina, is this possible. Do you think we might actually be able to get away from here?" Then, she seriously remarked to me, "Please don't give me hope if there is none."

"There is always hope, D'avia. I am hope." At that D'avia's eyes began to well up, but no tears fell. Neither girl actually had tears fall. They both shook their heads to rid their eyes of moisture when I noticed the bruise on the back of Mina's neck. She had a blanket around her shoulders, and I silently and gently pulled at it a bit. As it fell, I couldn't help gasping, then quickly covered my mouth. My eyes welled up. The bruises on Mina's arms were horrid to look at. I immediately wanted to kill the person who did that to her. I took her elbow with my left hand and her hand with my right bending down to kiss her arm. I did this impulsively. This time Mina's chin came up with a forced frown on her face because real tears began bathing her face. She gently hugged me. She hung on for at least a minute when

D'avia joined us and made it a group hug. We remained that way for a couple of minutes when, "Bang!" was heard somewhere outside through the brush. The next thing I knew, Mina, startled,was pushing past me and crawling out of the hiding place like a fast mouse. She covered the entrance, and I heard her yelling, "Coming Mama." We exited behind her but with stealth and hid in the brush close to the entrance to make sure it was covered.

Over at the roundhouse, "Where have you been? I was looking everywhere! You have your evening chores to do, young lady!" Then I heard a resounding 'slap' of a hand.

"I'm sorry, Mama. I'll go do them now," Mina yelled. What I did not hear were the sounds of a girl screaming from the slap.

"And, I told you not to go into the woods too far; you could get lost, and I am not going in there, you hear me!" her mother screamed after her while taking clothes down from a line. Her words sounded muffled, so I whispered to Hans, "How far away from her are we actually?"

Hans replied, "Not far enough. She is loud. But it is like the length of a golf course or more. You know a gold course?"

"Yes, I know a gold course," I smiled at him. "Are we safe here for now," I asked quietly.

"Yes, she won't come in the forest this far. Mina's mother is easily frightened and superstitious. You know, afraid of monsters and ghosts and that sort of thing," he rolled his eyes. We went back into the bunker.

Looking at the five of them, I almost forgot D'avia was to my right. I turned to her and asked, "Are you alright? Do you need food or anything?"

D'avia brought her knees up to her chest and wrapped her arms around them, "I do want food, but Mina brings me what she can. I'm always hungry, but I get enough from her to live. I just wish I could light a fire. But we can't. The smoke would draw attention. The lamp will have to do. I'm

96

cold a lot, but I've gotten used to it. I do cover myself with a lot of blankets, and sleep. That helps."

"Yes, I see. How was Mina able to get so many blankets?"

"Actually, she went near the military place where soldiers stay. She saw a bunch of these packages fall off the back of the truck. I guess nobody noticed her because she brought back four bundles. They turned out to be blankets for the soldiers. They are thick, so they are pretty warm," D'avia claimed as she fingered the edge of one of the blankets.

"Yes," I said, "wool is a very warm material," I commented.

"Okay, we have to go now!" Hans blurted out forcefully but quietly as possible. He startled me.

"What's wrong," I asked.

"Mina's father is off duty. He cannot see us. He sometimes walks about on the railroad yard tracks with a lantern, so we had better get back over the crossing before he suspects anything! D'avia, are you going to be, okay?"

"Yes, go, go. I don't want you to get caught. Please," she said looking at me one last time, "You are my 'hope'," she pleaded in a normal tone.

We surprised D'avia by hauling in a box of food: some cheese, cold meat, some bread, and cold milk. She looked like a child staring at a Christmas tree.

"Hurry," whispered Ada as she began pushing my butt toward the exit tunnel. "Hurry," followed Lian. "Hurry," forced Klaus. "Hurry," scolded Clotilda.

I crawled as fast as I dared without ripping the knees out of my pants. We emerged from the opening, patted down the bushes over the opening, and speed walked toward the railroad tracks.

He was down the line a bit, but Hans told me Mina's father had a habit of standing on the tracks and swinging the lantern around for a while on any track. Which meant he could also walk all the way down the track on the forested side of the rail yard. I walked so fast while making sure I stepped on pine needles to be quiet. We halted by the tracks we crossed, me out of breath. The children perched on their haunches peeked down the tracks and saw it was clear. Jumping over the tracks and down into a shallow gulley, we ran on the dirt road that led to a paved road.

We finally slowed our pace, walking casually into the square where our temporary home was. Few people were out and about due to the various curfews, so I strolled like I hadn't a care in the world, and drew no attention which is exactly what I wanted.

# Chapter XVIII

When we got back to the house, Lian made a one-pot meal which we ate ravenously with some delicious bread. I then asked to be excused and went to my room. I closed the door and sat on my bed and began to cry. I cried very hard and long. Although, I tried to muffle it, so the noise would not go beyond my door. Eventually, I laid down and continued to sniffle from my crying. I couldn't think about anything else except the hovel where the girls were, the dirt and root ceiling, the cold despite all the wool blankets, the dirty dresses the girls had on, and their smudged faces. This was suddenly reality slapping me in the face. At first when I got here, I was scared and nervous, but I began to ease a little as everything fell into place with the house, the job, and making our way to the hovel. But, once in the bunker, seeing those eyes that bore right through me as if pleading for rescue, I felt the danger in my bones. I felt their fear tangibly. I felt their desperation to believe I was their only hope. I felt their immediate trust that I would be their savior. The weight of this responsibility sat on my chest like an elephant.

Now I experienced a fear I had never felt in my entire life. This was real, very real, scary real, uncompromising real-not play-acting.

Softly, one of the kids knocked on my door. I sat up, wiped my eyes, and said, "Come in." Ada quietly entered taking delicate steps as if what she was doing was secret. She closed the door gently. As she approached the bed, she stared at me the whole time.

"Are you alright?" she asked softly.

"Yes, I'm fine," I said, "No, I'm not." And once again began crying stuffing my face deeply into a pillow. Ada rubbed my back for a few minutes while I cried and then stopped abruptly.

"Eves, sit up," she commanded. I did not respond. "Eves, sit up now!" she more forcefully. I finally sat up looking at her. She took my hands in hers and began, "You've done your crying. I understand. Now it is time to stop and face the situation with guts and determination to succeed. Remember we have been here before. We have seen failure in all its horror. We have this last chance to change that. We cannot afford for you to break down and tell us you can't do this."

I looked at Ada's eyes. *How is this possible? She is so adorable with her dark-haired bob and bangs. Yet, what comes out of her mouth is the maturity of an adult.*

"When you face all that, we have, you become 'street-smart' as you would say. Perhaps I never told you, nor did the rest of them. We are all orphans. We came from the Guttenbras orphanage here in Stuttgart. That's where we met and became friends. The orphanage had about 140 children of all ages living there. It is on the very north side of Stuttgart. There was some bombing over in that area but not much. Though the orphanage suffered enough damage that the military moved us to a grand house formerly owned by a Jewish family of jewelers. We already knew Mina from before the orphanage move because her mother used to come north to visit some sister or other relative once a week. Mina always had to stay outside and the orphanage was only a block away. She would see a bunch of us outside, so she came to play. We got to know her very well. Her mother could never leave Mina with her father or he would pamper her and She

100

would get jealous. That was not a good thing. That's why she hits Mina when she is upset. When they moved us, the five of us slipped away in the commotion. We hated it there. They gave us not so much food, and they were very strict. They made good use of the chalkboard pointer on our han."

I understood exactly what Ada meant. I asked, "How did you get all the way here to the west side of Stuttgart?"

"It is a long story, have patience while I tell it. Mina had told us her new address, but we had to find it. It is enough to say, it took us a few weeks and we still couldn't find her address,"

Ada stared into the middle distance, "Well, we had survived by stealing food out of baskets, and hiding in the back of empty houses. Of course, we broke in but we made sure there was no one in them. Many people, Jewish people, had been rounded up away from their homes, so there was food left in some, and blankets, and we found some clothes we carried in a suitcase we took. We even found some money hidden in cans. We could buy food."

I interrupted, "Where did you live while you were waiting to come get me?"

"Oh, we were very used to looking for shelter, and continued to break into homes unoccupied. Whole families were just taken out and shoved up on trucks. We thought ourselves fortunate for a short time until we found out the families were not brought back. Everything became for the taking, although now we felt bad. But more useful was the fact that we finally were able to take trams the rest of the way to this side of town. Thank goodness. It was exhausting walking so much.

Then we followed a truck once on abandoned bicycles. We found out where many of the Jews were taken. That is how we found Mina's address. The trucks divided taking some families to another neighborhood with a gate or to the railroad station. It was when we followed the truck to the railroad that we hid and sneaked a look at the station and saw soldiers separating people. We spotted Mina doing chores outside this tower. We were so excited to have found her, we ran to her and gave her so many hugs. Her mother caught us outside talking to her and screamed at us to go away, calling us bad names. She slapped Mina to the ground and told her never to talk to us again. That is why we love her and she loves us. We are her 'good family'. So, we have been to Mina's hiding place many times.

"I know you said you failed the first time you tried to get her out because you were only children," I sighed.

"That is right. It was just too difficult. We were without an adult, so we were too conspicuous even though some parts were successful," she paused, "in the end we were not. So, we came to get you immediately after we failed the last time."

"I see," I said, "You are extremely resourceful children. I guess I never really knew what 'street smarts' was. Wow, it's just like growing up skipping parts of childhood."

"One question," I asked, "How did you find D'avia?"

"Oh, my, we never told you that part. I am so sorry, replied Ada.

Ada took a minute to look down as if she was preparing to make a speech. Tears appeared in her eyes. She cleared her throat, then looked up at me and began, "After we found Mina, we saw that she was digging the hiding hole for herself to get away from her mother, someplace she could be by herself. So, we helped her. We fixed the ceiling so it wouldn't fall in and got her the blankets and all that. We would visit her almost every day, sit in a circle and play games together. We had to make sure her mother never saw us. Well, one day, we all decided to sneak over to a place from which we could see the train platform. We were curious as we saw so many people there with suitcases, families, and soldiers. We watched from under a railroad car that was standing at the end of the line. We had quite a good view. We saw everything. The soldiers were separating women and men, sending children with the women, being quite brutal if people resisted. We were shocked at the way the people were treated. We'd never seen anything like it. Then, one family came up to the soldiers' checking papers and the soldiers began separating them. One man clung to all of his children in a round grasp. There were three boys and a girl, and the soldiers began trying to pull them apart. The father swung his suitcase at a soldier and there was chaos where some other people began swinging suitcases at the soldiers. Right as the chaos was growing, the father, using his suitcase as a cover, pushed a little girl off the platform saying something into her ear, but we couldn't hear. He threw his suitcase down covering her. We saw her roll over the edge and under the lip of the depot platform. In the confusion, she crawled to the furthest side under the rail car from our viewpoint. We got her attention as she lay under the car and motioned for her to run toward us as no one on that side of the car was looking. She barely got to us when we heard the shot. She was with us under the rail car lying flat when she saw her father fall to the ground. Her mother and the boys plopped down by the man. Then an officer-his chest glittering with medals-drew his pistol. I watched in frozen horror as he shot her mother and each of her brothers where they knelt. D'avia tried to scream, but we all put our hands over her mouth and hugged her tight so she would not attract attention. You see, it became completely silent after that officer shot her family like that. We had to squeeze her between us while laying as flat as possible between the metal rails. Fortunately, there were so many soldiers screaming in a panic and barking orders that no one looked our way. We had to stay like that for an hour or so. We were afraid to move. Finally, the train began to pull away from the station and the soldiers began walking back through the building. We waited another ten minutes or so and saw a soldier pick up the suitcase D'avia's father had thrown. He set it on a trolley with other suitcases and left also.

Then and only then could we move. We were so stiff from staying frozen to the ground we had to move slowly to get up and Hans and Lian picked up D'avia so she could walk with us. She didn't even look at any of us. She just stared down at the ground and let Hans lead her away. When we got to our 'bunker', we liked to call it, she scooted down the opening and into the cave and scrunched up in a ball facing away from us as far from us as she could. She didn't cry or whisper or make a sound. We tried to talk to her, but she didn't move. We covered her with blankets. She stayed like that, staring down, for almost two days. Finally, Klaus brought a piece of paper into the bunker and stuck it in front of her face then backed away. She finally turned around. We couldn't believe it. She asked him what was on the paper! D'avia held it in her hand and sat up. She looked at our group for the first time and began weeping quietly. She placed the paper in her lap and showed us the picture on it. Klaus had drawn a picture of all of us in a group sitting with our legs crossed and fishing off of a log with her. We surrounded her and began touching her and hugging her. She started crying hard. We continued to hold her for a long time. Finally, Mina's mother was yelling for her and she had to leave. We stayed with D'avia until she fell asleep. We all left to get some food from the house we were in, but we left Clotilda with her so she wouldn't wake up and be scared. Clotilda fell asleep next to her. We brought food back the next morning. Once she started to eat, she asked us our names and who we were. She gradually started talking but always hanging on to one or another of us."

"Did she tell you about being pulled from her house with her family?" I asked.

"Yes," Ada commented solemnly. "And, now that they know, I will tell you what I told them."

"Will she be upset with you for telling me?"

"No, no, it would have been told eventually. I just thought it was the right time because of your weeping. We need you to be finished weeping and gather your strength. There is no more time for weeping or you will fail and be in much more danger if you are weak."

"I understand. I have lost so much in my life in my recent past. I thought nothing could get worse. I was wrong. This time is very much worse. I will try my very best. I will get angry if I feel like crying. I will clench my fists if I feel scared. I will do anything I can to have courage. I must not fail." I stared away in the distance and said, "I would give my life to save these girls."

"No!!" Ada grabbed my face in her hands, "You must not. That will be a failure. You must live. It is necessary that you go back to your time," Ada said looking startled. "You must succeed and live to return," she said more forcefully.

"Okay, okay. I will, "I said as I put my arm around her on the bed.

She kissed my cheek and told me to sleep well. Tomorrow was another day that needed my resolve. Fortunately, after crying, I always slept well. It exhausted me.

The next day I was up and left for work on my own this time. When I arrived, my basket was full and I began immediately. Herr Berchtold was not present at this desk. However, I heard arguing out in the hall. It got louder as it got closer to our door. I could hear two people arguing in, what was to me simply a thick German accent, yet I could understand every word. Herr Berchtold appeared to be yelling at another officer I saw through opaque glass. The other officer had a higher voice that almost made me think he was a girl.

"You will do as I say! Get those Jews into the area provided for them! Do I make myself clear?" Berchtold yelled.

"But, my Colonel, it is overcrowded which may spread disease to our guards," said the young man.

Berchtold screamed, "Then we will delouse them before shipping them out! They were supposed to be moved two days ago! I have a schedule to adhere to. Do you understand?!"

"Yes, my Colonel." With that the young man passed the door shrinking away.

Herr Berchtold came in the room seething and sat at his desk piled with papers. I did not look at him, I just continued typing. He had his hands on the desk as if he was going to push it away. However, I took a peek sideways and saw that he was calming himself down with deep breaths.

Finally, I heard, "Sorry, Frau Obermardt. I hope that argument did not offend you too much, the language."

I turned and starred directly into his eyes and replied, "I consider it none of my business." I turned back to my work. Now I was getting upset about what was said, but held on with the control I could muster.

"Good girl," he promptly replied. I decided I wanted to throw up. "Good girl"? What am I five?

The days were spent working, getting coffee for Herr Berchtold and others. The 'coffee' was not pleasant. I sipped the bitter liquid. It didn't smell like real coffee, nor did it taste anything like real coffee. It left a bitter taste that was barely tolerable. I suppose, because it was made out of some ration-era concoction of roasted acorns and oats. I also drank tea, which they still had at the office. However, I found out some senior personnel tucked away real coffee in their secret hiding places in their desks in the office.

I continued to work and made myself unremarkable so I could fade into the background of the office. I was afraid someone would see my expression and ask what was wrong. Thus, I tried to keep an impassive flatness to my face. During this time, I also stole moments to study the maps on the walls, taking notes, and rifling through Herr Bertold's papers. Many women worked in the outside office, but I kept the door closed for the most part and listened for any footfalls. Some of the women talked animatedly with the passing officer's laughing and such but it was obvious that the joviality could change in a second and that the men were in charge.

One night we decided to make another foray to Mina's hideout. We followed the usual path, the usual way, and had no problems getting into her bunker. She and D'avia were eating out of cans. Mina was supplementing D'avia despite her meager dinner at home. She had done her chores and was allowed to be out until her bedtime. Since she was 10-years-old, that meant

9' o'clock to 10'oclock. Since it was only 6'oclock, we had plenty of time to spend with her. The children played a quiet game of cards. I decided to crawl out and observe anything I could in the house. I stood but bent down and snuck into her mother's garden shouldering my way around the back of the house to get to a window. Fortunately, the curtains were thin enough that I could see in. Still, I stayed at the edge. Mina's father was a big burly guy but only about 5'8". On the converse, her mother was a thin scrawny woman about 5'6 or 7" in a black dress and an apron.

# *Chapter XIX*

Mina's father was eating, his back to his wife as she was washed dishes at the sink. She dropped a plate with a loud clatter. The father looked up straight and pounded the table so hard that I jumped. His wife, however, shuttered violently.

"How am I to eat in peace with you making so much noise!" he sputtered in a scream with spit catapulting forward onto the table.

"I'm sorry, dear. I'll be quieter. I promise," she stuttered not facing him.

"Get me my beer. I'm going to sit and read the paper!" Everything he said he yelled like a commandant.

"Right away," she mumbled.

I saw him stomp out of the room into another room. I just starred at her as she turned around to get him his beer. She was probably 35 years-old and looked 50. Her face was a permanent frightened frown. A pang of unexpected pity struck me. She was trapped, just as much a victim of this man as Mina was-but in an era that offered her no escape. And yet, she took her own misery out on her child.

I crept away silently and moved back toward the hiding hole. Arms wrapped around my neck and squeezed me until I couldn't breathe. It was Mina and D'avia.

"I was so scared you wouldn't come back! Even though Ada said I had nothing to worry about," Mina whispered fiercely as if she was on her last breath.

"I know, I know. But I will always come back. You have to trust what the group says." I patted her on the back, so she would let go affording me the ability to get fully into the hiding hole. Hans asked us all to sit in a circle so we could hold hands to pray. Praying was new to me but I didn't mind. After the prayer, Hans said that we needed to start planning. So, we sat there with each person staring at me to begin.

"Ok," I said, "Here's the beginning of the plan. I work in an office where my boss is in charge of transportation, moving people, a good many of them Jews and the people in charge of moving them must carry specific papers listing names which show who they are loading and what their destination is. I haven't been there long enough only two weeks, but I only have a month, since what I've heard about officers are becoming fearful that the British are going to step-up their bombing on Stuttgart. America is joining the fighting as well as the air strikes. The city has a lot of industry here, ah, factories that provide supplies and machines. I have to get you all out of here within the next two weeks. That's an incredibly short goal. I've managed to blend into the walls..." D'avia interrupted and said, "What do you mean you go into the walls?" Lars leaned over and said, "She means that she is not paid a lot of attention to in the office."

"Oh," said D'avia poised in a contemplative manner. Then, "That sounds good." She gave us a small smile for the first time I ever saw her change her expression.

"Again, I have blended in and I've been doing my homework when Herr Berchtold is out of the office. He has maps hanging in his office on two walls. I have studied both. One is a large map of the city with its designated Jewish 'ghetto' areas. It was written on the map. Oh, sorry." The children did not understand why I apologized. They all looked at me with question marks on their faces. "Oh, um…, where I come from to say a person lives in a ghetto means they are usually poor, not well educated, and often black."

Mina said, "What is black?"

"A person who has a dark brown skin color," I replied.

"Oh, well I have never seen such a person," replied the two girls.

"They're very special people. However, this ghetto has Jewish citizens crowded into a few city blocks with a gate to keep them in. Never mind let's move on. There is also another map of the whole of Germany and most of western Europe. I studied that one and took some notes. Since you five have told me that our goal is to get to Switzerland, I checked routes and how many miles it is."

"What are miles?" This time coming from D'avia.

"Stop interrupting, we'll explain when she is finished," admonished Lian.

D'avia went quiet. "It is alright, D'avia," I said, "Miles are used in America. Europe uses kilometers. I am sorry. I was about to tell you how many kilometers, but first I had to figure out miles, so I would have a good idea how far it was. You understand?"

Both girls nodded their heads in unison.

"Alright, now," gathering my thoughts, "I have one best route we can go. We could take the train from Stuttgart to Konstanz. It will take about three and a half hours. We could transfer to Switzerland's train, but I think this is too risky. Here's where it gets sticky." I stopped and looked at them all to see if I was going to get another group of question-mark faces. None, so I continued, "I think I can get a staff car with the paperwork to travel on a weekend to the farm country outside Stuttgart. Although, I have to have a very good reason. I think I have Herr Berchtold's trust now, sort of. But I have another plan to secure that trust as a more protective demonstration so

110

he will feel obligated to see me as a female who needs his help." Again, I looked at their bland faces. "Let's move on. You don't need to know all that. Anyway, I've done so much paperwork there already that I have typed up many Permissions for Travel documents for citizens to move throughout the country. A few were even for soldiers sent to the Swiss border so they could check on any trouble at that end. However, I found out that while the Swiss soldiers don't particularly like the Nazis, they are not interested in permitting any Jewish people to cross their borders. This is what they told the soldiers. I can hear much when Herr Berchtold is on the phone or discussing such information in his side meeting office. He does close the door but not all the way and I pretend to be working while my ears are zeroed in on the conversation. Fortunately, if I close his office door, it is quiet, so I can concentrate." The children were looking at me with rapt attention. My eyes scanned their silent faces and I continued, "I hear quite a bit, a lot more than he thinks I hear. I'm sure of it."

"So, what do you think about the way to get past the guards at the border?" Hans asked.

"I will not take you past the guards at the border." Everyone's eyes enlarged till I saw the whites of their eyes.

I stated, "We are going to have to walk for a while after drive from Stuttgart to Kontanz. I will dump the car in the woods near the station. I can't take the risk of them finding the car at the train station. From there we walk.

"Isn't that going to be dangerous to catch a train?" Clotilda asked.

Hans said, "Shhhh, Clotilda, we listen first. OK?" Clotilda settled down but remained anxious as I continued, "I have traced a few towns that the train stops at. So, I want to get permission from Herr Berchtold for me to visit the country one Sunday just to get away from the city. If he lets me go, I will take one of the staff cars with a Permission to Travel voucher only as far as the train station in Stuttgart. There are five trains running, so I have to determine the best route for us. He may have someone follow me, but I doubt it. He doesn't pay a lot of attention to me. Once I get to it, I will assess any difficulty getting on the train, being checked, guards, anything like that. So, my plan so far is to ask for another Sunday visit to the country in two weeks, hide the car, catch the train, and we get off the train at the station by Lake Constance. From there we have to get a boat to cross the lake. We can only do it at night. I need your help because I can't go that far ahead of time. And, we will have to ride across the lake as quietly as possible until we get to the Switzerland side and we'll be across the border. We will have to walk from there. But then I must find people who will help Mina and D'avia." I was exhausted from talking so intently. I sat back against a mud wall, and just took time to breathe.

"How do you know we can find people who will help?" asked Mina.

"All of Switzerland is not like the border guards, the military, nor the government. We still have a lot to do though. We have to get better clothes for Mina and D'avia," I answered.

"I can take care of that," said Clotilda and Lian at the same time.

"Then there is food to prepare. We will have to make many sandwiches and bring something to drink for all of us whether it's wine or beer. Milk is too hard to keep fresh," I foretold.

"What about the fact that there are so many of us?" asked Mina.

"Big families are common everywhere, Mina."

"So, seven kids won't be noticed traveling with you?" asked Mina.

"Maybe, but I will queue you as to when to become a nuisance, so that the conductors and other passengers avoid us to get into another compartment just to get rid of us!"

"Clever," mused Hans, "But how are we going to make D'avia look un-Jewish?"

"We're going to change her name and fix her hair into pig tails, but I have to lighten her hair first with lemon juice. I have to find a lemon first," I answered.

"How are you going to do that?" That was Ada.

"You all are going to have to help me. Search the market, search some of the vacant houses. Can you?" I asked.

"Yes," the answered in unison.

"But, what name would you want, D'avia? It has to be a non-Jewish name."

D'avia looked at me with her eyes scrunched up and said, "Can I be Heidi? I heard that in a story."

"Absolutely, my girl! And what about a last name?"

Hans rolled his eyes at me, "We are your children. We have to have your last name!"

"Oh, right." I was so tired at that point; I just wanted to lie down and go to sleep. "Um, my name is Obermardt. Try it out."

Ada started, "H-m-m, Ada Obermardt, Hans Obermardt, Klaus Obermardt, Lian Obermardt, and Clotilda Obermardt, Then there's Mina Obermardt, and Heidi Obermardt,!"

"But," Mina hesitated, then asked, "Who's going to believe you have seven children all of same age?"

"You are so smart. I thought of that. Okay, everyone, line up by height," I ordered. The kids all scrambled to crawl into order. Fortunately, they could stand up, but I couldn't. Their heads met the roof of the bunker; whereas I had to remain seated or on all fours.

"Alright, by height we have Hans, Ada, Lian, Clotilda, D'avia, Mina, Klaus," I reported, "M-m-m, well, Hans, you will pass for 15, Ada, you are 14, Lian, you are 13, Clotilda, you and D'avia don't look that much different, so you two are twins and 11. You will be fraternal twins. Mina, you will be your real age 10, and, Klaus, you are small so you will pass for nine years. Everybody agree?"

"What's 'fraternal'?" Mina asked.

I answered, "Clotilda and D'avia were born at the same time, but they don't look exactly alike, as identical twins would. That's as simple as you need to know."

Klaus was in a pout, "I don't want to be the youngest!"

"Well, it is sensible because you are the smallest," I said.

"But I'm really 11!"

"I know, sweetheart, but your ages have to make sense with so many of you. Please don't give me a hard time on this. I know you're smart. But you must be nine for it all to fit."

"Klaus always gives a hard time. He often wants to be the boss," Hans said, "Settle down, Klaus, or I'll sit on you! You have to do what we need. We all have to do what we need to help, Cully or Eves Obermardt. Got it?" Hans looked at Klaus with arms akimbo and a deadly serious stare. Klaus pointed his pout at Hans but didn't say a word.

"Well?" asked Hans, "Are you going to cooperate or what?"

"I just don't like it. I never get to be the boss," he commented.

"Now, you're acting like a kid," Ada said.

"I am a kid, but I'm not 9!"

Ada added, "But what's our goal, Klaus? Have you totally forgotten? What's wrong with you?"

"He didn't get any sleep last night. Bad dreams," said Clotilda eyeing him, "He refused to sleep. He was scared."

"I was not!" Klaus defended.

"Klaus!" I shouted. He whipped around and looked at me as if I was his mother scolding him, a little nervous.

"I am going to take you home to bed with some warm milk. You are going to go to sleep and get your rest till you feel better. I know what it's like to feel out of sorts," I said even toned.

The children all nodded. Despite Klaus' precociousness, he wasn't acting himself and didn't look 11 years old.

"Before I take you up, Klaus, I am going to invent your birthdays. They will be your real birthdays, except for the year. Can you all memorize the new year of your birthday and your age?" I smiled, "I will have it on my papers."

All the children said their 'yes'' nodding at each other, even Klaus.

I proceeded to figure out on a slate Mina had to give them all their ages and birthday year. Mina spoke again, "Still who's going to believe you have seven children?" She looked at me with a slight fear in her eyes.

I said patiently, "Mina, you have limited experience in a typical family life. You have been isolated by your mother for almost your whole life. There are many families in Germany with seven to eleven children or more depending on how long a couple has been married. It is not unusual for a mother to have a child for every year she is married. Not unusual at all."

D'avia spoke up energetically, "I have three brothers and no sisters," Then she looked horrified and began to sob in her lap. I quickly went to her and held her stroking her back. I held on tight so she would feel secure. D'avia cried for almost thirty minutes. I just rocked her and stroked her hair. The other children sat quietly the whole time and waited. It was remarkable how much patience they had at their age, but then they were 'street wise". They had survived rough treatment in their past and had struggled to keep their demeanor non-reactive holding back any display of emotion on their faces. I believe they felt for D'avia or they wouldn't have led me into this situation, but they kept a tight hold on showing what they felt on the outside as a defense to get through this, their mission. *How sad,* I thought. *And criminal that made them need to do that.*

That night, after we left the girls, Hans made dinner, another one-pot meal, but it was very good. The crew hit their beds being so exhausted from the events of the day. I took Klaus to bed with some milk I had warmed. When he was tucked in, he apologized to me and was asleep two minutes after drinking the milk. Looking at him ached in my heart. I wanted to keep him safe too. I kept thinking that he was just a child. But I knew better. He was a mystery of child and adult who came to get me. I was the only one who had to get up in the morning for work so off I went to my room.

I got to work on time the next day having left the children still sleeping. The children sleeping looked like beautiful angels as I checked on each one before I left. Hans had been up already, of course. He was the recognized leader of this band of operatives and, thus, was getting food ready for breakfast.

At work, the routines were same-o, same-o. The noise from the women's typing on huge machines and the noise from telephone operators in another long room with no door dominated the room. I went to my boss's office, captured a cup of tea from a small space made for such things, and approached my desk. For some reason, my glasses fell off. Quick as a wink an officer who had just entered the office picked them up and held them out to me. I thanked him and turned to sit down. But he didn't leave. Strangely he leaned over my desk and violated my 'personal space' staring into my eyes.

"Frau Obermardt," he started, "how would you like to join me for dinner tonight?"

I backed away on my chair a bit and replied, "I'm not really dating right now. I'm a widow with seven children."

He persisted, "I know, but it has been a while, has it not? You need to get out and relax, have some fun, and it would be such a waste not to with someone as beautiful as you." He said in a mellifluous voice, I hated to admit.

"I'm sorry, Herr Richter, but I'm very busy right now," I said trying to look away from his face so near mine.

"I don't think you understand, Frau Obermardt," he insisted, "I do not get refused when I ask a girl out," he smiled devilishly.

I smiled right at him, "First of all, I am not a 'girl' and secondly, I have seven, that's seven children to look after. I don't leave them alone at night."

He stood up firm and straightened his uniform. His expression changed to one of steel determination, "I understand your oldest can look after the others in the evening. I will pick you up at 7 o'clock. Just give me your address."

I wanted to stand and slap the guy, but I was afraid to with circumstances of not being sure if I would get in trouble for doing so. I thought feverishly about what to do when Herr Berchtold entered the office. The officer addressed him and turned back to me.

"I will come by later," he said. He reported something to Herr Berchtold, yet Berchtold was eyeing me. My face went pale, I suspect and I went into a mental panic, so I looked down. Then, Herr Berchtold paused what Richter was saying by holding up his hand.

"I've seen that look before," he said. "I suspect Herr Richter is known to be somewhat of a ladies' man. I'd be careful."

"Sir, I did not agree to have dinner with Herr Richter. I have seven children to care for and he would not accept 'no' for an answer. I did not slap him, but I wanted to. I did not know if I would get in trouble for doing so," I appealed to him.

"Really," he surmised, "A good worker and a good German mother. So, you have no interest in him at all, and you say he forced himself on you for a date?" Herr Berchtold stood their holding some papers and was turned sideways towards Richter. He looked at me like he was weighing the situation. I waited patiently behind my desk resting my arms in my lap, hoping for a resolution to the situation.

"Colonel, it would not hurt her to have a little reprieve from work and minding her children. And she would have a good time," gestured Richter with an arm extended for good will.

He turned away and placed the documents on his desk. Immediately he came to the front of my desk. Looking down at me, hands at his sides, he said, "Frau Obermardt, you do excellent work and have a commanding presence about yourself that shows as confidence. I admire that."

"Thank you, Herr Berchtold."

Then Berchtold startled me by grabbing Richter's arm, turning abruptly and leaving the office with Richter in tow. I just went back to work determined to calm down with deep breaths while I began on the documents from my basket.

The day went by rather quickly which I was grateful for and I closed up my typewriter preparing to get my coat off the rack. When in rushed Herr

Richter stomping into the office and marching right up to me grabbing the upper portion of my arms in his. It hurt. I was frightened. I couldn't swallow.

"How dare you tell Herr Berchtold that I 'forced' myself on you. You are a secretary, you are not important here, you are a nothing!" His face came closer, "You have done the unforgivable!"

"Herr Richter!" bellowed the approaching Herr Berchtold, "You will take your hands off of my assistant now!"

Herr Richter raised his hand to slap me. He was in a rage. Herr Berchtold quickly stepped toward him, swung him around brutally and slapped Herr Richter backhanded across his face. I was frozen. I couldn't move but had my mouth opened in an 'O'. Herr Richter had gone down with the slap. He scuttled up and wiped his bleeding nose. There was a lot of blood dripping on his uniform. I saw that Herr Berchtold had a large gold ring on his right hand. It was quiet, very quiet. The typers outside of the office had not stopped typing with all the noise in their area. Another officer entered the office quickly.

"Hermann, what happened. What is going on?" he asked startled and eyed Richter firmly.

"General Konig, sir, Herr Richter has violated personnel protocol of this office in the most heinous way," he answered starring at Richter's bleeding nose and mouth. "I filed an order request for him to be moved to supervising the troop movements at the office in Reim. It is quite an honor to supervise our fighting men." He never took his eyes off Richter, although Richter was staring at the floor still trying to stanch the blood."

"Richter!" said the other officer, "You will join me in my office to determine where and when you will go." Konig turned to Berchtold. I will decide where Richter will go. I will find a field position where he can use his officer skills to the best of his abilities. I will arrange for him to leave as soon as he is packed and in field uniform. However, Colonel Berchtold, I value your suggestion," said General Konig with an air of superiority.

Konig walked toward the door with an understanding sneer toward Richter. "Come Herr Richter, now!" he commanded.

I was still frozen in place. Herr Berchtold approached me and put a calming hand on my shoulder. He asked if I was alright and then said, "I apologize for Herr Richter's insult to you Frau Obermardt. It shall not happen again. Is there anything I can do to calm you and make you feel safe?"

*Bingo*, I thought, "Well, I was thinking," I said hesitantly, "if I could take a staff car and visit the countryside this Sunday for a picnic?"

"By yourself, Frau Obermardt?"

"No, I want to enjoy reading a book on cooking while my children played."

He seemed to be pondering the thought with his thumb up to his lower lip. It took some moments as I waited.

Then abruptly, Berchtold nodded his head approving, "Alright, I see no problem with that. I will need to see the book before you go. You can bring it in tomorrow," Berchtold said off handedly. "I will give you a pass for the staff car and make sure you have your papers on you. You are not going too far, I hope? There are bombing runs that land outside the city right now."

I wasn't sure if this was a question or a warning, so I just replied, "As soon as I see a cow or a goat, I will know I'm already there," I assured him. Herr Berchtold laughed, and simply said, "Very good. I wish I had time to visit the countryside. But I think you can use a little sojourn with your children.

With that, I left for the day.

# Chapter XX

When I got to the house, Hans had been cooking because I was used to eating at American time for dinner. He greeted me while one of the other children set the table. I watched as they were all busy doing something: washing dishes, helping to cook, even dusting the furniture.

"What's with dusting the furniture, Ada?"

"We have to make the living area clean," she said, not looking at me, like I was an idiot.

"I see, and did you clean at the orphanage?" I asked.

"Half of all we did at the orphanage was cleaning. We scrubbed, we washed windows, we swept floors and the front and back porch every day. You should have seen the size of the front porch!"

Klaus came in the room. "We are leaving after we eat, Frau Obermardt."

"Shouldn't you practice calling me mother?" I queried.

"Umm, I suppose so. But I will call you Mama."

"So, will I," said the other kids at the same time.

"I think the sooner you get used to it, it will become natural. Also, when I come home from my work, you each need to approach me and tell me your name and your new birthdate, understand?" I said this as I collapsed on the divan. I was so tired from work and from the emotions I exerted that day. Each child responded near or far that they would do so starting the next evening. I then told Klaus, "I am not going tonight, Klaus. Can you tell the girl's I'm very tired, and I need to sleep? Oh, and bring them some more bread and cheese tonight. Also, I managed to sneak some chocolate out of Herr Berchtold's private supply." I said all this from my slouched position on the sofa. I reached into my purse and brought out three chocolate bars. "You shall have to share, Klaus. This is all I could get without him becoming suspicious."

Klaus approached me looking at the chocolate in my hand like it was gold. He starred at it until I asked, "Klaus? Klaus? Are you alright?"

Klaus slowly put his hand forward and took ownership of the chocolate. He treated it delicately, taking it to the dining room to show the other children. Their eyes went wide, the whites showing all around. They were very quiet. I entered the arch to the dining room and saw that all of them were staring at the chocolate.

"What is it? Is something wrong?" I asked.

Lian turned to me and said, "I have never seen chocolate. I have heard of it, but I have never tasted it." The other children were nodding their heads murmuring together.

"Okay," Hans said, "Let us sit and eat and we will discuss this after dinner." Everyone sat down and ate ravenously not making a sound other than slurping which I didn't mind at all.

After dinner, the children put on their coats and checked each other. They turned to me as Klaus said, "You going to be alright here alone?"

"I believe so," I assured him. His concern made me feel tender toward him instead of apprehensive. He had been so curt and stiff with me before.

"Well, lock the door, turn off the lights, go to your bedroom. Only have one light on or a candle might be better," he counseled me.

"I will, Klaus. I promise. Do you have what I told you to bring?"

"Yes, I am better at deciding that than you." Then, "I mean don't worry. I will take care of the food for them."

"Sounds good, Klaus." I put a hand on his shoulder in affection. He stared at my hand then looked at me a little uncomfortably. "I'm sorry, do you not want me to touch you?"

"I am not used to receiving affection from anyone."

"In that case," I surrounded him with my arms and gently gave him an open hug. He was a little stiff, although, I felt that with more exposure, he might like it. The rest of the children stared at me soundlessly. Therefore, I approached each one and gave them a gentle hug. Again, the stiffness. While their arms remained at their sides, they did not resist. I could tell by how surprised they were that none of them were used to affection of any kind. *How sad.*

I opened the door for them making sure it was dark behind me and whispered to them all, "You're going to start getting more of that."

The children looked at me speechless other than waving good-bye with the whites of their eyes showing completely.

I proceeded to go upstairs and retire. I did as Klaus suggested and just lit a candle, got into my bedclothes, and wished I had a book more interesting than the cookbook I had to show Herr Berchtold the next day. I started snooping around. I checked the side table, the dresser, the wardrobe, the window seat. Nothing. I looked under the bed, up the fire place with the poker. There all I got was a splash of ash that made me cough. Then I decided to check the wardrobe again in case there was a book hiding in the clothing. To reach the shelf above I stepped up on the floor of the wardrobe which sounded strange, perhaps hollow. I stepped down and got on my knees examining the floor of the furniture. I knocked on it and, sure enough, it sounded hollow. So, I looked for a way to lift it up and saw a thumbhole in the back left corner. I lifted it and the whole bottom came up from the back. Moving some of the clothes aside I still couldn't bring it up. I tore clothes off the rod and threw them on the bed. I finally brought up the wood and found not one, but several books lying neatly spread out two-layers thick. I brought my hands to my mouth and stared in awe. The titles. I couldn't believe it. Leather bound books such as *Huckleberry Finn*! There were several other classics of writers from Europe and the U.S. *The Great Gatsby, Native Son, For Whom the Bell Tolls, Stars on the Sea, Pride and Prejudice, Jane Eyre, Great Expectations, The Pickwick Papers,* and poetry from writers in France such as *Le Crève-Coeur (Heartbreak).* I figured the woman who normally lived here was well-educated, could read English and French, and had left Stuttgart to avoid the war. *Perhaps she had information.* I knew these books were banned in Germany and had been subjected to the book burnings.

Who knew, but these books were a miracle giving me something to read during our downtime. I just had to retrieve one at a time and then put it back with my bookmark. I couldn't risk leaving it lying around. However, I was very excited to be able to read in order to lull me to sleep which is exactly what I did.

About midnight I awoke feeling curiously odd like something was not right. I put my robe on and walked in bare feet to check on the children. Their rooms were empty! I couldn't believe it. I didn't know what to do. It wasn't like I could call someone looking for them. I dare not go out alone to Mina's underground hiding place. I was too unsure of myself. The children's presence always made me feel safer. *What to do*, I thought. When I realized there was nothing I could do, existing in an era I only read about but was truly a real threat to myself. A cold stark terror gripped me. I was truly trapped here. I had no idea how to return to my own time. I took a couple of deep breaths, checked the door lock on the front and back doors, and decided to just wait it out for the six hours till I had to get up for work. I had to go to work or Berchtold would be suspicious. I couldn't afford that. So, I sat against my pillow on the bed and tried to read. I read the same page over a dozen times. I couldn't concentrate, thus I just sat there humming to myself and staring at the bedcover listening for any sound.

I performed the next day at work, a perfect pantomime of normalcy, while panic clawed at my sides. I kept as busy as possible, praying the whole time that the kids were alright. I tried to suppress the panic I felt by working quickly and double checking everything I had done. Before I knew it, the work day had ended. I did not rush to get ready to go home. Herr Berchtold was not present in the office, so I just left.

When I got home, the children were there! I was so happy that I started to cry. They ran to me and I hugged all of them crying while they muttered their apologies.

"Where have you been? I was so scared," I scolded them.

"Frau Obermardt, we have a story to tell you, so come and sit down. We are alright, and we are so sorry for scaring you, but we had a bit of a problem last night. So, sit down on the divan or couch, whatever you call it, and we shall start from the beginning," Ada counseled me. Thus, I wiped my eyes with a handkerchief and sat down to listen. The children sat on the floor in a semi-circle around me.

"Okay, do we all agree Hans should tell her?" asked Clotilda.

"No, I think Klaus should tell it. He's better at that stuff," said Ada.

"I can tell it," said Hans.

"Really, Hans? You know I'm better with details than you are," Klaus commented.

"Alright, alright, go ahead," Hans pouted.

Klaus sat silent preparing his thoughts and then began."First of all, we had no trouble getting to Mina and D'avia. It was when we tried to leave that the problem started. It was a very quiet night and we must have been too noisy carrying our laughter through the trees or something. Anyway, when we went to leave, we snuck out but made the mistake of thinking we could just walk upright in the forest leading away from the bunker. Mina's mother had secured a flash light. And pointed it up to about 10 feet from where we were walking, but she heard us. She blew a whistle and we ran. However, there were already soldiers at the edge of the forest who started chasing us. Maybe two or three. We almost made it to the train crossing when one of them caught Lian by the back of his coat collar. We four fell to the ground on the other side of the tracks since it was dark. We didn't move and listened for Lian.

"What are you doing in the forest this late at night?!" demanded soldier #1, holding Lian up and shaking him as if he was being hung. Lian must have just stared at him because we heard nothing. Then a slap was heard by all of us. We wanted to rush the soldiers, but we couldn't afford to sacrifice any of us. So, we waited. Finally, Lian said, he was just playing in the woods hunting.

Then soldier #1 asked Lian why was he playing at that hour. There was a strict curfew for children. Lian finally told him that it gets so boring at night, so he goes out to play. Then the soldier asked him where he lived. Soldier #2 and #3 were looking around for us with their flashlights but didn't see us. We did not move a muscle pressing our faces into the leaves to stay hidden. Then we heard a slight rustle in the brush, and stones began flying in the air at the soldiers hitting them everywhere. Lian was dropped and ran over the tracks to us. The stones kept coming; the soldiers couldn't even hold their flash lights. They used them as shields to their faces. Suddenly, they just ran away from where we came from. We still didn't move. Lian was now on the ground by me. Slowly, the sound of rustling leaves grew closer. Two boys about 15 or 16 crawled over to us. They motioned for us to follow them crawling. After, like two minutes, they said we could stand up. They never spoke, just kept motioning for us to follow them. So, we did. We walked what seemed like a mile, but it was just to the other side of the woods away from the house. Then, we went into an empty barn. It was locked but they had a way of crawling through a hole. Inside we found a group of older boys and a couple of girls. There was only one lantern lit in the middle of the barn. The people looked at us, and the boys who rescued us told them what happened. A couple of the boys came up to us and told us that we were safe for the night and could sleep in one of the stalls on the side of the barn. They gave us some bread and cheese to eat. Also, they gave us some beer to drink. We laid down on straw and fell asleep immediately because we were tired from and trying to calm down from our scare. When we got up the next morning, it was early and the people gave us apples to eat! They were so good. Then they asked us where we came from and we told them that we were orphans trying to run away. The biggest boy told us which way to head and they gave us some food they wrapped in a cloth plus one jar of beer. I asked them who they were to save us and help us. A girl walked up to our group and said "We are *Edelweiss*." I asked her what that was. She and another boy told us that they were teenagers that hated the Nazis and were trying to make as much trouble for them as possible. One boy, Lukas, told us that they were like the 'underground' fighting the Nazis, but they were all teenagers. Well, we thanked them a lot and then told them we had a mother we actually wanted to return to and asked how to get to our street. One of the girls told us that she would take us. So, we left with her and here we are. Except, we had her drop us off at the corner so she didn't know what house we were in. They saved us. I thought Lian was gone. But we would not have let him go without a fight. We were just glad *Edelweiss* came along. I didn't think of throwing rocks. I feel so dumb."

"Oh, stop, Klaus. None of us did. Just be glad that those kids came along," said Hans, patting Klaus on the back and smirking at him.

# Chapter XXI

**T**he next day at work I had brought in the cookbook I was going to study on my weekend away. I waited to catch Berchtold in a spare minute at his desk. Finally, at 11 a.m. I walked over to his desk and cleared my throat because his head was concentrated close to his desk top writing. He jerked his head up and saw the book in my hands. I offered it for him to peruse, but he barely glanced at it, and waved me away mumbling, "It's fine. I really didn't need you to bring it in. I often quote protocol without thinking. Go back to your work."

"Yes, sir. Can I have just a moment to ask you something?"

He averted head, "What, alright, I'm very busy. Go ahead." He appeared to be thinking and half listening to me but I began.

"I was thinking more about making my little visit to the country and wondered if it wouldn't be more convenient to find an inn out there. I could go Saturday and return Sunday midday. I just think it would less stressful than going and having to come back in the same day. Does that pose any kind of problem for you, Herr Berchtold?" I inquired.

He returned his straitlaced gaze to my face, frowning. I held my breath. He lowered his eyes onto his work as if he was back to focusing on its issues, but he nodded and said, "Sounds like a much better idea. I hope you have a good rest, Frau Obermardt." And, with that, he turned back to his work.

A little while after 12 p.m., a host of men entered the office and headed directly for, what I call, the conference room. They clicked their boots marching straight to the table and assembled around it standing until Berchtold stood and entered. He hesitated, then turned around and said, "Frau Obermardt, don't let anyone bother us. I mean no one, understood?"

"Of course, sir."

With that he closed the door gently and all the men took a seat. Berchtold sat at the head of the close end of the table. *It seems shuffling papers is part of their important business.* I could sneak a peek while filing and the discussion went on for quite a while. After maybe two hours, the conversation became heated and I could see from my typewriter that men were getting cross with other men and yelling began. Berchtold pounded the table once more. I heard Richter's name mentioned from a portly officer looking straight at Berchtold. Another officer further down the table appeared to be chastising the portly fellow. Then all hell broke loose: there was shouting, two men rose and waved their fists at each other. Some sat back sedately. The argument seemed to be between portly guy and the other two across the table. Then the tone changed, everyone calmed down. But suddenly portly fellow pointed a finger at Berchtold, shaking it towards his face. Berchtold remained calm and just stared at him from what I could see. Unexpectedly, I started as General Konig entered the office without knocking and strode straight for the conference room. I kept my nose down and side-looked at the action. Upon opening the door, all the men stood and saluted the general with the requisite "Heil Hitler!" and remained standing. The general waved for them to sit down, he closed the door behind him and took the seat at the far end of the table from which a subordinate officer hopped out. The talk began again. General Konig addressed each man who responded to him. It remained calm and I got back to my work. It seemed like the more I completed, the higher the 'In' basket remained. I sighed and just kept plunking away. A few minutes later, the door of the conference room opened and I could easily hear the men thanking Colonel Berchtold except for the portly fellow. As the men filed out with various files in their arms, portly fellow raised his voice slightly to General Konig saying, "I object! Richter was needed here. You changed his orders over a silly secretary?"

General Konig said, "Watch your tone Hemlich! This is not your concern. You're just angry because Colonel Berchtold defended his secretary. Of course, Richter was adept at his work, but, unbeknownst to you, Hemlich, I have had more than a few complaints from officers who work directly with the girls in the nest out there. I need the personnel in the nest, every last one of them. I don't want any of them to suddenly turn up ill because of Richter. He will serve well where I sent him."

"Colonel Berchtold has no authority to hang on to one particular secretary. She should be put out in the nest!" the portly fellow bellowed.

"She is the best assistant I have ever had in the three years I've been here, Hemlich. I can and will keep her if I want!" Berchtold sneered at portly fellow.

General Konig had had enough and put his hand up, "I order you to 'stop' right now, both of you." The men were silent for a moment, then Konig said softly and deadly, "Hemlich you will try my nerves one last time and I will send you out into the field to be effective. Colonel Berchtold has done an excellent job ridding us of the Jews into those ghettos and onto those trains for the camps. I will not endanger his prowess at such effective management. Is that clear enough for you?"

The portly fellow snapped his heels and raised arm for his salute to Hitler, then left the office abruptly.

"Thank you, General Konig. You honor me with your evaluation and your support," Berchtold softly stated.

For the first time I saw, General Konig stepped very close to Berchtold's face looking calmer, "Don't make me regret it, Colonel Berchtold." With that Berchtold saluted the general as he sauntered away. I thought that was unusual Berchtold being so angry, but I believed he was trying to calm down after the brouhaha. Berchtold grabbed his coat and hat and told me was leaving for the day. He instructed me to lock his office when I left. I was surprised because he never told me to lock it before. *Oh well,* I thought.

That Saturday, I left the kids at the house. I did not want to draw attention to us in a staff car, and I did want to stay the night at an inn with five children. It would be suspect if I brought all the children. Thus, I gave them their instructions, only they really gave me mine, and with that, I set off. I had procured a car from the motor pool. It was quite peculiar to be driving a 1940s German military staff car, but it was kind of fun to figure out too. I allowed myself a few brief thrills from the driving this car. As for the trip, I headed west to the country with my coat and gloves on due to the chill. Once I got out of Stuttgart, the country was beautiful with its hills and flat lands, winter grasses, and green pines. It took the better part of an hour to find an inn. When I did, it was quaint with its white decorative wood trim which seemed more Swiss to me, but I don't know cultural architecture. I drove up and exited my car with my small case. When I entered the inn, a lady at a desk asked me if I wanted food or a room. I told her both, and she showed me to the most charming room I had ever seen. It personified the word 'cozy'. I asked if she could bring the food to my room to which she, "Of course." I was so tired and didn't have time to scout around that day. I went to bed and awoke from a beautiful slumber I hadn't remembered having in a very long time. Eventually I came down for breakfast with some town folk populating the inn as well. I heard my name called. It was the barman holding out a phone receiver to me. "You have a call." I took the receiver a little hesitant not knowing who knew where I was.

"Hello."

"It's Hans. You alright?"

"Yes. How did you get this number?"

131

"You told me where you were going. There're only two inns on that road. I asked at the post office. They told me how to get telephone numbers. I told him I had to get a hold of my aunt. I said my uncle was sick and I needed my aunt to come home. So, I asked him to help me. He was very glad to help me. Most German people are actually pretty nice."

"Very good, Hans. I'll be home late this afternoon or evening. I want to do a little reconnaissance of the trains, the schedule, and the Swiss exchange train. I'm taking the train from here to the border and back. I can observe the changing from one train to the other process. I have to be back by tonight to return the staff car.

"Okay, be careful. Just act natural."

"I will, Hans, I promise I'll act even if I don't feel it."

I took a look at the train schedules at the local station and determined there were several choices to go East, not so many to return. Therefore, I figured out which one I had to take in order to catch one of the ones returning. I wouldn't be able to look around at the Swiss station as much as I liked. However, it that worked out smoothly. I was surprised of what I was capable.

I drove back that night managing to get the car within the parking slot on time. Immediately I started for home. The buses weren't running this late, so I had to hoof it. What a long walk, ugh. I got to the house around midnight. The kids were waiting up for me. They had wanted to go see the girls that night but realized it got too late by the time I arrived. Klaus asked how the trip investigation went. I replied, "We can't take the train." Their faces were all question marks. "It's too dangerous with seven children. There were guards everywhere at the border on both sides. They were checking passports for forty minutes. I can't risk it."

Clotilda spoke up, "Well we'll have to figure something out. We're going, no matter what."

"Yes, we are, Clotilda. I just have to observe and think. Okay? I have to go to bed. I'm exhausted and I have to get up early tomorrow."

"Good idea," said Lian, "You look worn out."

Klaus jabbed him with his elbow. "You don't have to tell her she looks bad. That's not polite."

"Sorry, Cully."

"No! You must call me Eves so no one makes any mistakes. Alright?" I insisted.

"Of course. Sorry, Eves," he chimed.

The next morning, I entered the office of Herr Berchtold and quickly put my things up heading for my desk. Suddenly, I felt someone behind me and turned with a jump.

"You startled me, sir."

"Sorry, I didn't mean to. I wanted to ask about your trip to the country. Did it help you refresh you," he inquired with a steady stare at my face?

I tilted my head to get out of the line of fire from that stare and answered, "It was very nice. I really used my time well to relax and read my cooking book."

"Good." He turned with a crisp click of his boots and entered the conference room. Then he stuck his head out and told me he was expecting four other men, listed them for me and asked me to go to his right bottom drawer and take out a package which had real coffee grounds in it. "Would you make coffee now for these gentlemen, bring in the pot and cups, then return the bag to the same place in my desk.

"Of course, Herr Berchtold, right away." As I strode to a small kitchen area, I made the coffee. Hans had showed me how coffee was made back then. I took a ceramic pot full with cups starting for the conference room.

However, I left a small cup for myself behind a binder shelf. After I returned from my delivery, I smuggled my purloined coffee and quickly took it to my desk. The first taste was different from modern coffee but so much better than that other mixture they made. So, I reveled in each sip.

That evening, we visited the girls using our skullduggery to approach the bunker. Hans whispered to the inside first, so we wouldn't startle the girls. Only D'avia was there. She said that Mina had to go do more chores and didn't want her mother coming after her into the trees. I told her that her mother was scared to go past the barrier log only a few feet into the forest. Mina said the mother was slowly creeping in further and further like she was daring herself to not be afraid. So, Mina is more alert to her mother's actions and checks the area around their garden to make sure her mother is not outside. She further reported that she and Mina are beginning to get anxious and frightened that her mother might actually come to close. I said that we would keep an eye on her and while I was working, I asked the kids to take turns coming during the day to keep D'avia company to which they readily agreed.

"I'll go first," said Klaus, "because I'm the smallest and can spy around the mound without being seen."

"Okay, you're a good spy, Klaus. See how your size is an advantage sometimes."

Klaus smiled with pride. Yet, I told him not to take any chances and to be very, very careful.

"I know how to spy, Eves. I'm a kid."

"Point taken," I patted him on the shoulder.

Now, I told them all in the presence of D'avia, that I was going to get the duplicated passes tomorrow at work while Berchtold was out in the morning.

"Are you ready?" asked Ada.

"I have a feeling something is brewing because I hear bombs going off in the distance. I think the Allies are having trouble or something because they don't seem to drop them closer to the city center. It's scary but they're either exploding miles away or there's days without any bombing. My instincts are pretty good. I just know something is coming soon with Berchtold having all these meetings. I heard something mentioned about lessening or increasing the control of the numbers of Jews on trains. I'm not sure which. I'm going to really try to overhear anything I can."

The next week Berchtold was out of the office in the mornings and I purloined as many blank copies of passes I could so I could practice filling them out without making mistakes. I didn't have to worry about passports because children weren't issued them. Just passes. That afternoon a bomb hit, metaphorically, when Berchtold returned to the office. He came in the door with a worried look. I tried not to notice and kept my head down. However, he strode over to my desk and told me he was being transferred to France to oversee the Jew camps there and to try and set up a few 'special' camps. I asked what a 'special' camp. He replied that it would not be necessary to know the details right now. I asked when the transfer would take place. He reported in two weeks. He also said that I would be granted a weekend's leave to go to the area to find suitable housing for me and my children. Although he did ask if there was any one who could take them in Stuttgart, I told him the children go wherever I went. He seemed satisfied with that and said I wouldn't have to leave until the weekend after next. I told him I understood. That was that.

He had another meeting that day and was talking about clearing out more of the ghettos to the trains. I heard that there would be a 24-hour schedule to transport Jews as quickly as possible. The men were trying to coordinate the details pointing to a map on the wall. I was furious, peeking up at them, as if they were discussing produce.

That evening, Thursday, as we visited, both girls were there. They looked alright, but D'avia was wearing thin. Mina said she had days where D'avia didn't want to eat; she was so scared to be left alone. I looked at the kids and asked what happened. They were supposed to take turns keeping her company. They said they were, but couldn't stay all day. Mina was gone more and more each afternoon and that's when D'avia was the most scared. I asked if they knew why. Klaus told me that Mina's mother had her doing more cleaning in the house and fetching things at the market. Mina would always eye the bunker off into the woods. She knew where it was from that distance. She even saw one of the boys looking around the side of the log even though it was so far. She waved anyone down after she made sure no one was looking.

It was late afternoon. Mina began telling us that her mother said she spent too much time in the forest playing and she had to help her out more. When Mina tried to quietly protest her mother slapped her so hard, she hit her head on the floor and became dizzy. We also noticed a few bruises on her upper arms. Then we heard screams in the distance.

I snuck out of the bunker leaving the children behind and went to spy on the commotion occurring at the train depot trying very hard not to make any noise and creeping slowly north of where we were. The commotion was getting louder. As I got closer, I could see soldiers arguing with the Jewish passengers. Women were screaming being separated from their husbands and causing quite a riot. There were hundreds of potential passengers and what looked like a shortage of soldiers to funnel the Jews into lines for boarding boxcars. I dared to get closer by elbow-crawling on the ground and keeping my head low. I found a small bush from which I could make a space and put my head partway through to see what was happening. The screaming and yelling were rising in tempo. Suddenly, it stopped when I heard a shot. Something fell from the air to the ground. I thought it was a doll until I saw a soldier grab a baby out of its mother's arms and angrily toss it in the air shooting it like target practice! I had to cover my mouth from screaming out loud. My eyes could not believe what I saw. It happened again. Another officer who walked up to another mother, ripped her baby away from her and with all his power threw it high up into the air and fired at it. The baby came down to the pavement but I looked away in time. There was a hushed screaming I could hear coming from the Jewish people. I dared look back with tears washing down my face. With my hand still across my mouth, I pushed my whole head down into my sleeve and screamed as loud as I could over and over. I screamed so loud the vibrations in my head gave me a splitting headache. I looked up to see the Jews doing exactly what they were told with no more resistance, no talking, and looking only straight ahead as the lines moved.

I inadvertently looked at the depot platform and saw a soldier picking up the babies shot by their legs and putting them in a bag. I simply could not believe what I was seeing. My eyes would not stop weeping. My hand would not leave my mouth.

Finally, I realized I had to calm down and crawl backwards to where I could stand and walk in a crouch back to the bunker. When I entered the bunker, I let out a sob so great that Ada covered me with her body and forced my head into her skirt. I sobbed for at least three minutes, but I had to stop. I had to get a hold of myself. I patted her arm to let her know she could let me up. I blew my nose in Hans' handkerchief. The kids were quiet and staring at me.

"We're leaving tomorrow," I managed to croak out.

"Do we ask what happened?" It was Hans.

"Not right now. I'll tell you later. Mina, can you go right now or will your mother be suspicious?" I asked.

"Mm-mm. I'm not sure, but I can't go back to the house and pack anything. My mother spies on me everywhere in the house."

"You won't need anything. Hans and the others have a bag of clothes for you at the house. Same with you D'avia. You two are coming with us now!" I was determined.

Dusk was approaching, but I didn't care. I instructed the children to crawl on the ground and follow me and Hans. We only had to stop once when we saw her mother come out of the house and make some noise throwing an axe into the ground over and over. I thought she was crying, but I couldn't be sure. When she went around back into the house, we took off fast crawling trying not to get punctured like I had or to get scratched by forest debris. When we reached the opposing tracks that we always had to cross, I encouraged the children to crawl up the incline, roll across the tracks and slide or roll down the other side as quietly as possible. We had to stay in this location until nightfall since the children were so dirty from crawling. When we dared to moved, I told them to stand and brush their clothes off as well as they could. Then we surreptitiously walked across a park instead of on the sidewalk. We maintained a consistent but slow pace. It seemed like eons until we got to the sidewalk we had to take to get to the house. Fortunately, I think, there was a new curfew due to the renewed bombing now by the Allies even though they were still off the factory positions. When we got to tall houses that served as apartments on the block, we walked alongside the wood or brick as closely as we could while moving forward with determination. Finally, we approached our block. I stopped the children and stepped away from the last building to look and listen. I heard a car in the distance but nothing near us. Thus, I hurried the children along more quickly until we got to the stairs to the manse we were occupying. Once Klaus unlocked the door, we entered single file, closed and locked the door. I told the children not to turn on the lights, but feel their way up the stairs. During this stealth maneuver, I went to the kitchen by feel and drank an entire glass of water. My throat was so sore from screaming. I then followed the path to the stairs and climbed up to my bedroom. The children were gathered on the floor. I took a breath and spoke to them.

"Alright, this is what you are going to do without discussion. Girls, I want you to go to the bathroom and draw a bath. I want each of you or all, whichever, to get cleaned up. There's plenty of soap and more towels in the hall cupboard. No more than fifteen minutes. That's all you've got. Boys, I want you to go down stairs and start making sandwiches. You can light a candle on the chopping island which is low. You will make two for each of us and pack them tightly in the wax paper and bag down there. Lian, I want you to get the beer bottles and a bottle of wine out of the basement and, save two of the beers for each of us. Can you open them? Well, Klaus can help you. There's a sewing basket in the living room. By that time the girls will be out of their bath and in their pajamas. Girls, you will then go down and empty the sewing basket onto the fireplace in the back. Line the basket with wax paper several times and put the sandwiches, beer and wine bottle in there. They should fit. It's a large sewing basket." I paused.

"There's two layers in the basket," said Clotilda, "We can put the bottles in the bottom and the sandwiches on top."

"That's good. While the girls are doing that, Mina and D'avia, you don't have to go downstairs; you'll just get lost. I want you two to go to bed and get some sleep."

"Which bed do we take," asked Mina.

"Anyone you want, but you and D'avia stay together. Okay?" I added.

"Boys, you will come upstairs and fill the tub again and wash up whatever way you want. Take the dirty towels and put them in the back of the cupboard. Grab fresh towels and get done. Into your pajamas. I want the girls to sleep in the same room. See if you can squeeze into the bed together or two at the top and two at the bottom. Got it?" I looked at them.

"Got it," said D'avia.

"Boys, same thing. All in one room," I reinforced.

"Got it," answered Klaus.

"Now go! And make as little noise as possible. It's late. I don't know when or where the patrols are coming around. But I don't want to take any chances. And, no lights. Use a candle if you need to. Hans knows where they are."

"We'll be the best," Hans solemnly said.

# Chapter XXII

**I** left for work the next day with all children up and dressed packing clothes that Klaus and Ada had retrieved from several abandoned apartments they managed to break into. Fortunately, they found a suitcase here and there, so they could pack the clothes. They also found a knapsack that they used for other essentials. The sewing basket worked efficiently.

I had to leave to go to work and make everything seem as normal as possible. I got to work and, seeing saw a flurry of activity, slid into Berchtold's office and to my desk. Only moments afterward, he entered focused on an open ledger. I tried to seem inconspicuous and I shuffled some paper into my typewriter. No luck. He turned sideways and acknowledged my presence with a nod and then went straight to the conference room. I did my work and, at half passed twelve, Berchtold came over to my desk.

"Frau Obermardt, I need to discuss something with you," he said succinctly.

"Yes, Herr Berchtold."

"Come into the meeting room. I'll be right back."

I immediately went to the meeting room, taking a chair near the door. I had no idea what was going on or was I caught? I was a little fearful. When he returned, he lay some papers on the table and a map making a few notations on both.

"Now I begin. I am being transferred west to convert one of the other camps in France into the special camp and to coordinate movement of the Jews in the surrounding camps to that special center." He looked at me stone-faced, so I kept mine the same. I will be leaving in one weeks' time, and I want you to join me. I can make provisions for an apartment for you and your children. I also can provide for movers to move any necessary furniture; however, there are apartments there that are empty due to our policy of relocating Jewish families. So, what do you say? I value your work and your professional presence. You are efficient and effective. The most important two qualities I admire. Any thoughts?" He asked tersely.

I took a breath and paused to look down and think. I wanted to give the impression I was considering the situation. Then, "I believe that would be a good move. I can keep my job working for you. My children will mind, but they are children. They will do as I say. However, if I could leave this week, I could find my own apartment, with your authority, and you could concentrate on your upcoming move."

"Of course. I am glad for this response. As I said, you will put your affairs here in Stuttgart in order and prepare to leave this weekend on the train. There will be no unnecessary fuss. We plan, we transfer." With that Herr Berchtold pushed a paper over to me to sign as an acceptance of the transfer, receive the travel papers, and a map that would show exactly where we were going to be stationed in France so that I could look for lodgings in the homes nearby. I took what he offered and left the room before him, to return to my desk. I knew now our plans demanded the children and I leave that evening.

That afternoon, as planned, Ada called and said she was really sick and needed me to come home. The children did not leave the house during the day because they were not in school. Records were too dangerous. I approached Herr Berchtold's desk solemnly and waited for him to raise his head. The phone rang, he raised his head, saw me and put up his hand while he answered the telephone. It was a brief call to which I only heard Berchold's quiet assent in response. He hung up the phone and lifted his eyes to me waiting.

"I really hate to ask this, Herr Berchtold, but my daughter is being sent home from school with a fever. I need to pick her up and take her home. May I leave to go get her, or do I need to quickly find a sitter?" I looked pensive on purpose. As Herr Berchtold took his time processing what I said, I stood still feigning this demeanor.

"Yes, I think that would be alright. I have another meeting elsewhere this afternoon." He paused looking out at nothing. "No, that will work out just fine. You may go. Our German youth are very important. We can't have one getting too sick. However, we have two more days of work before you leave for France." With that he lowered his head and went back to work. I immediately grabbed my purse and my coat steadily moving to the door of the office. Herr Berchtold did not look up, so I left without another word.

I went to a coat closet for the staff and looked for a couple of small coats for women. Since it was still early afternoon, they would not find them missing until six p.m. I folded my coat over them until I headed for the exit and put my coat on, or it would have looked suspicious going out into the chilly air without it. I kept the other coats close to my body, head up, and walking swiftly through other busy staff in the foyer. I headed directly for the staff cars and showed the outdated permission slip I still possessed casually to the guard, with my finger over the expiration date. He waved me on knowing who I worked for and directed me with the keys to my car. Once I arrived home, the children, pleasantly surprised, were ready to go almost immediately. I had a few things to pack for which they provided me a battered suitcase. I packed only warm clothes, men's pants, and one woman's suit with hat. I was ready to go.

The car was out behind the house in an alley. The children were packing their stuff into the trunk with several blankets over it in case we were detained for some reason. Suddenly, we all jerked violently at the sound of a bomb going exploding on the outskirts of the city. While Hans said they missed the munitions factory the Allies or whoever were trying to hit, b they were getting closer. Hans, like many street kids, knew his city As we took off in the car at a mild pace, we did see people running for cover. Klaus pointed out the smoke in the distance, but Hans said that if they hit the munitions factory it would have been a much bigger explosion. He continued that he thought it was because of the constant cloud cover over Stuttgart that they had yet to get it right.

I drove west out of town following the train tracks that left Stuttgart behind. I tried to follow the route the train passing was taking parallel to the road I was on. I lost it at one point and had to take a back road to get closer. Fortunately, the back road actually went somewhere and was not a dead-end. It was a long ride for the children, about 2-3 hours during which they looked out the window or slept, leaning on each other. I encountered little to no traffic except for a farmer in a truck. Soon, I was able to rejoin the paved portion of the road when a troop transport was coming the other way. I told all the children but three to sit on the floor. I was relieved when no one seemed to take notice of our car moving at a steady pace while I looked straight ahead but using my peripheral vision. I was heading for the town of Konstanz on the east side of the Swiss border. Lake Constance was designated as a border between Germany and Switzerland. I picked up the train tracks again in the distance and kept moving. I had plotted out the route, copying what I needed from Berchtold's wall maps. I yearned as I drove to see the blue of a lake.

Then, there it was. We came over a small rise and I saw the lake in the distance. I had to divert to a secondary road to head into Konstanz. I knew it was a resort town besides a fishing village. I didn't think many people would be resorting at this time of year, but I wasn't secure in that guess.

Next, as we entered the city proper, I told the kids to peek out the windows looking for boatyards. While they did that, I scanned the area to find a place to hide the car. We had crossed the tracks where all passengers had to disembark to climb onto the Swiss train that left from there. But I couldn't risk taking seven children on a train especially as it was getting dark and crossing the Swiss-German border with seven children. I would cause too much circumspection. I pulled onto a side street and all the way to the end where there was little to no activity in a residential area. The boys opened the trunk and we ate sandwiches in the car, drank a weak beer, and ate apples I had bought. Night was falling faster and the streets were quite empty. I dared to start the car up and drove slowly without the headlights on toward the lake. Liam called out, "There's some boats!"

Everybody whispered a loud "Sh-sh-sh-sh...." to him with fingers poised over their mouths. He hung his head, but Clotilda gave him a squeeze and said, "Chin up, you spotted it."

I drove past the boat yard and parked in the darkest side road I could find. I told the children I would be right back. I had to check out any boats we could use to get across Lake Constance. Lian objected and said he was smarter and knew some about boats he learned from an uncle. Even though the uncle didn't want custody of him, he visited for a couple of weeks one summer and learned about boats when they went fishing. That was up until he had to return to the orphanage. His uncle had said he was sorry, but he couldn't take the responsibility for a child as a bachelor.

I hesitated since I knew about boats, but, in truth, modern boats. So, I let him go with several 'Be careful warnings' from everyone until he rolled his eyes.

"Are you done?" he asked everyone. He climbed out of the car and darted into dark spots on the road to cross under a light at the boat yard. I didn't know what he was doing but got so antsy I was beside myself. It must have been ten very long minutes when he arrived back at the car scaring everyone when he opened the door.

"Okay, there are fishing boats with a cabin and rowboats with big oars. The boats with cabins will bring attention. So, I think with so many of us, we need to take one of the bigger open boats with the huge oars. Two of us will have to row at a time."

"Good. Now how do we get the boat into the water?" I asked.

Lian looked impatient with me. "I'm not stupid. One of the big open boats is tied up to a pier."

"Sorry, Lian. Now, we have to figure out how to get all of us over there."

Hans then talked, "I think we should follow Lian in groups of two. We won't get into the boat until we are all over there. Then we need to sneak into the boat in a line. I suggest all of us except the rowers lay on the bottom of the boat with the blankets and luggage over us. Although, I think it's too dark to go now. There's a moon tonight, but it's behind clouds."

"What do you suggest?" I asked. "We can't wait until morning and be seen," I pleaded. Hans starred at me contemplating. "As soon as the moon moves from behind the clouds, we go."

"How do we know when that will be?" Mina whined. Up till now, I had almost forgotten she and D'avia were with us. They were so quiet in the back. No one spoke.

Then Klaus said, "How about we take the blankets and move our suitcases while there is no moon to a boat up on land. We can tuck them under an overturned boat. Lian, are there any like that?"

"Yes, about half a kilometer away from the water," he answered.

"Ok, then that's the plan. As soon as the clouds drift away from the moon, we move," he finished.

Our group executed this plan like trained soldiers to me. Their ability to sneak across the road and slide our things under the overturned boat was impressive. Although, we did have to spread blankets out because the ground was cold. I had to lay down due to my size while the others could crouch. We didn't have long to wait. The moon began peeking out of the heavy cloud cover. As soon as light could be seen, the boys got busy and propped up the side of the boat with a stick and the girls shoved our things out from under. The moon was coming out full now, so we quietly picked up everything among all eight of us and walked silently in a string down to the parked boat. The boys loaded first while the girls handed the provisions down to them. Lastly, after the girls, I stepped down crouching so I wouldn't fall overboard. Although, we found that the boat was big enough for all of us. *Good, good, good, good*, I thought. Hans untied one end while Liam untied the other. They took rowing positions as I crouched at the front as the lookout and the girls and Klaus lay on the bottom on top of some blankets and the luggage covered by more blankets. I estimated it would take about forty-five minutes to cross the lake. Therefore, we used the moon as a guiding light so we didn't have to use a lantern. However, about ten minutes from the other side of the lake, the moon moved behind a dense cloud leaving us in pitch black. We continued on in the straight direction I initially aimed the rowers. The trip was agonizingly slow. We eventually hit ground. I asked everyone to stay quiet until I checked around to see if there was activity of any kind. Once assured it was all quiet, I had the children disembark. I told the kids from here on that we had to walk until I could get to a farm to ask for information. So, for the night we walked until we found an old shed that seemed unused on the side of a bushy hill. Staying there for the night, we slept comfortably in our clothes, huddled together under a dozen blankets. Even though the girls wore skirts, their woolen stockings kept them warm.

# Chapter XXIII

The next morning, we awoke just as the sun was reaching a quarter of the way up in the sky. I looked at my watch and when I saw it was nine in the morning, I shushed everyone and crawled to peek between the boards of the shed wall. There was quite some activity as people were setting out with their fishing boats and others opening shops. Apparently, Konstanz, the town ran into Kreizlingen on the opposite shore, so there was enough activity to provide me with cover as I proceeded to move out of the shed behind a building and survey the area. I was hoping I could find someone to talk to about where I might find shelter for the Mina and D'avia. I decided to be brave. Opening my suitcase, I pulled out the suit I had brought, heavy stockings, and low heels. I fixed my hair and took a deep breath before heading out.

"Where are you going first?" asked D'avia.

"Not sure, sweetheart. I have to see who I can approach to find out information."

"Where do you think you should go first? Wouldn't it better if I came with you?" asked Hans.

I glanced at him and replied, "Maybe so. It might look more natural. Yes, come on Hans, get your coat on and we will go together."

"I already have an under shirt, a shirt, a sweater, and my coat." He said confidently.

"Oh, I wasn't looking. I'm trying to see where I can go first. A shop, the boat dock, or just have us all walk out of town toward the fields of a farm," I pondered.

"I have an idea," said Mina, "Why don't D'avia and I walk to the shops or people on the street and see if there are any Jewish areas in the town? After all, we are children and people with either laugh at us or want to tell us where they are. Then again, they may want to ask us why we want to know," talking more to herself than us, "but I think, maybe, it would be easier for us to approach a person."

"Why do you think that, Mina?" I asked.

"Same reason we couldn't get here all the way," Klaus answered.

I looked at him quizzically with my face all scrunched up.

"We're children, Eves, I mean, Cully, I mean Eves. I don't know what I mean," said Hans, "Children are less of a threat when they approach an adult. And, since Mina and D'avia are kind of cute, it would invite more curiosity. Don't look at me like that, Klaus."

Lian fell on the floor of the shed laughing mimicking Hans' description of 'kind of cute'. I think Lian was overtired because of all the rowing and which led to hysterical laughter. Ada and Clotilda punched him playfully to stop him from laughing. Before I knew it Klaus, Mina, and D'avia were all on the ground trying to stop Lian from laughing. Except, his laughter became contagious and all the kids were laughing. I stood there like a homeroom teacher waiting till the laughter died down.

"Are you done now? It's great to see you laugh, but we're not done yet," I smiled, "Okay, I'll risk it, Mina. You and D'avia go onto a street and feel out if you can approach someone. *D'avia didn't look as clearly Jewish anymore since I had put lemon juice on her hair mixed with a touch of peroxide.* Make sure they look 'ok' to approach. Don't approach a man right now. Let's stick to a woman."

"Okay," they said at the same time and that got the laughing going again. I was rather surprised after all we'd been through that these children could still laugh so easily. But I was glad.

The girls went out on their venture and we, in the shed repacked the suitcases, to relieve ourselves of the rucksacks. It didn't work. Instead of using suitcases, blankets and clothes had more room in the rucksacks. The boys could shoulder them. But we did manage to pack Mina and D'avia's belongings into one suitcase.

Everyone sat around on a blanket and waited. No one felt like talking. Klaus and Lian closed their eyes again as did Ada and Clotilda. I thought that Mina was very brave for going out on the street and told Hans so.

"She is a master manipulator. How do you think, despite the bruises she maneuvered around her mother to hide D'avia?" Hans eyed me; eyebrows raised.

"You're right, Hans. I have learned a new appreciation of how strong children had to be during this era. How independent they had to become. How self-sufficient some of them are like your lot. I doubt many of the kids in my era at this age could stand up to the reality of what these kids have had to do. I know they couldn't. Since the end of the war, modernization came fast in America with all the new appliances, housing, and such. Kids were beginning to be more protected in the new system of suburbs. It makes me shudder to think if my kids ever had to go through something like a war on home ground."

Hans covered my hand with his. "You are here now, Eves, and your children did not have to go through this war. Be grateful for that."

I held Hans' hand and looked at the dirt-filled creases in his skin. I bent over and kissed his hand. He did not pull it away. I looked up at him and saw of look of compassion. I also felt sad that these children had to miss their childhood by trying to save the lives of other children only because of a religious difference. One that most children didn't acknowledge in their play relationships. Mina and D'avia returned from their scouting. They entered the shed with strange looks on their faces. I couldn't tell if they were successful or had failed to gather information.

"Well, what?" I stammered.

Mina looked at D'avia and smiled then back to me. "We got information about a community of people that are part Jewish and some who live near the Jews who have no problem with them living where they do."

D'avia said, "She was very friendly. I got scared a little when she asked if I was Jewish, and said, 'Yes'. I wanted to be honest. That is what I am."

"She said we could go out of town to the west and then a little south. I have the directions in my head. Anyway, there's a farm or something with a few people on it that will give us directions. The lady said they won't hurt us," Mina finished. Mina's eyes were so big as she was talking to us. It looked like excitement. I couldn't tell, but I knew she never cried about us taking her away from home.

I clapped my hands, "Okay, how do we get ready?"

"We carry the suitcases," piped Clotilda.

"We'll carry the food basket. Well, should we eat first? I'm starving: we haven't eaten since yesterday," asked Ada.

"Yes, we should eat the rest of the sandwiches and the apples if you want. Then we'll divide everything to carry between all of us and walk out of town to the west. I didn't realize that we are already on the west side of town, so we won't have to go past a lot of businesses or people. We'll go through the grass behind buildings to leave, to be on the safe side," I informed them.

"Who's in the lead?" asked Klaus.

"What does it matter?" asked Hans.

"We could just walk in two's," expressed Ada.

"I like walking in two's," added D'avia.

"What about me? I don't have anyone to walk with?" asked Klaus, "Just because I'm the smallest I get left out."

"Oh, I'm sorry you got stuck with me," I complained.

Klaus turned a bit red in the face, "I didn't mean it that way. I just wanted…." I cut him off before he went on further,

"I know what you meant, Klaus. You can walk with Hans and Lian. Happy?" I inquired with a smile.

"Thanks, Eves. Can I guys?"

"Of course, you can, you dopa," Hans said as he cuffed him on the back of the head.

I suddenly noticed how more relaxed the kids were. There statements, the move of their bodies, and their eyes. I could tell the distinct difference of a lesser fear. They felt safer. They looked safe. I made them safe. I felt a burst of pride in my chest for having helped accomplish this. I got them to relax by getting them to a safer place. I was happy. And, with that I caught the suitcase Hans held out for me to carry. We set off west and out of town after I changed the heels for my oxford shoes. We walked for a long time. But we also passed people who were bicycling back and forth as well as a few people of mixed ages walking. The occasional vehicle passed; however, we did not encourage attention nor indicate we wanted a ride.

Aebischers Farm was printed on the sign we saw walking up a gravel road. I hurried in front of the group to halt them before we walked any further.

"Okay, please let me do the talking. Remain silent and obedient. Hang together and follow me. Got it?" The children all nodded. As we approached the farm, white washed house on the left, dirty red barn on the right across a dirt path that probably served as a driveway, I waved at the two men standing in front of an open area of the barn. They did not respond but looked my way.

"Hello there," I said as friendly and cheerful as I could, desperately hoping they would understand me since we weren't in Germany any longer. As we moved closer, we stopped at a respectful distance and I inquired how the gentlemen were.

"Hello, how are you this beautiful day?"

The older one looked at me skeptically at first and then switched to a friendly stance and answered, "We are just fine. And you are right; it is a beautiful day. What can my son and I do for you?" The son did not look as open to us in his stance and a furrowed brow.

"I was told in town that you might know of the orphanage in this district." I said with confidence.

He eyed me and then answered, "Well, ah, there is about ten kilometers maybe twelve down that secondary road, he pointed, and then you take a right at a sign that says *Kinderdorf Pestalozzi.* It is a large building with many orphans named after a Doctor Pestalozzi. That is all I know. But it is an alright place. A few children come by the village occasionally with supervision. They are well-mannered, so the women must care very well for them. May I ask if you are going to deposit more children there?" He pointed at the children behind me.

"No, we are looking for my other son, a twin for this one," I pointed at Ada, "My husband came here on holiday to fish with my son. When the war started, he left my son with some kind people, so that he could return to Germany and get the rest of us. He did not like what was happening in Germany. He did not return to our family. We do not know what happened to him." I hoped I sounded convincing. *No, I am praying earnestly that I sound convincing.*

"Well," the farmer replied, "it is very likely he could be there. I don't know where the children come from. I hope you find him." His voice took on a tinge of sympathy. By this time the son turned toward us in more of an open manner.

"Thank you very much. May I know who to thank for the directions?" I inquired.

"I am Thomas Schmid and this is my son Peter," pointing to himself.

"It was a pleasure to meet you. Thank you so much for the information."

He took off his cap and nodded, scratching his head, "You are very welcome. I hope you find your other son," he replied with compassion in his voice.

"Me too," I said as I turned around to leave, the children in tow with our luggage and crate of food stuffs.

"Wait! Can you come back for a minute?" he called out.

I got a little nervous but turned with the same gaiety I demonstrated before, "Yes, what do you need?" I began strolling back to him. I told the children to wait where they were.

"I wanted to know if we might give you a few bottles of milk for the children. I have four I could give you?" he offered. I didn't know what to say. His generosity was not something I encountered in my time in Germany.

"Uh-," I looked at the children who had their hands together as if they were praying at me. "Yes, that would be exceptionally nice of you."

"Peter, go to the barn and get four bottles out of the cold box for them." Peter nodded dutifully and asked, "Should we give them five? One for the Missus?" Thomas seemed to pause to think. "Yes, maybe five. We have another milking to do in the morning. We should have enough for deliveries." Peter took off toward the barn.

"This is again very kind of you Herr Schmid." I panicked. I didn't know what I should address him as. *Would 'Herr' work or what?* He didn't seem flummoxed by this, so I stood there waving the children to come closer. Peter returned with five cool bottles of milk and handed each to one of the children. I turned to thank him again when I noticed Peter had run away toward the back of the barn. I was just going to thank Herr Schmid again when out came a battered truck.

"My son has some milk to deliver. He can drive you about half the way to the children's home place, but no more. He must turn a different way for his deliveries," he raised his eyebrows looking for assent.

"That would be most gracious of you. Are you sure we aren't interfering with his work?" I asked sweetly.

"Not at all. But remember," he wagged his finger, "only about half the way. I am sorry he can't take you the whole way. He must make his deliveries," the farmer lamented.

"It is still wonderful," I replied.

The children began loading their suitcases and packs and the milk onto the back of the stopped truck. Peter had jumped out to lower the tailgate. He also helped the children get on board and sit on the floor. Peter paid me particular attention and brought out a short stool for me to step up to the truck back. He also held my hand like a gentleman to assist me. I almost felt elegant right before sitting on the rusted floor of the truck.

We waved to the farmer as Peter drove off and he returned the farewell gesture. Peter drove in silence the whole way as well as the children and I. Although, the children were also silent because they were sharing the milk. The other two were put away in one of Hans' back satchels. It wasn't very long before Peter slowed to a stop at an intersection of dirt and gravel roads. We unloaded our things and I made sure to go to the window while the children stood at the side of the road.

"I wanted to thank you so very much Herr Schmid for the ride. It was very kind of you," I uttered.

"It was my pleasure Frau Obermardt? I heard you introduce yourself to my father."

"Yes."

"Alright, follow this road another three or four kilometers and you will come to the sign my father told you about," Peter said kindly. We waved him good-bye and started our journey to the orphanage. The walking was not so bad because we could walk on road instead of bumpy ground.

When we thought we could not go another few feet with the luggage and sacks, even though the children were trading off who would carry, we saw the white back of a sign coming toward us. We tried to walk faster and eventually rounded the sign. We arrived! We all were smiling and yelling 'hoorah' swinging the luggage around.

"Okay guys we still have to walk the road to the house," I said soberly. However, the kids sped up their steps faster than I could and gained some ground ahead of me over a hill where I could no longer see them. When I crested the hill, I looked down the path and saw an enormous three-story Swiss-style house with three balconies on the front. There was no formal driveway up to it and no formal lawn but a wide array of plants, weeds, and trees. I didn't care. I walked forward in awe at the size of it. Some children out front ran over to my children and started gabbing at them while I looked for an adult. I didn't have to go far. A woman of middle age came walking out quickly as if to protect the children from advancing soldiers.

"Can I help you?" She was flailing her arms about walking so fast.

"Yes," I assured her, "I was looking for the proprietor of this home."

"Well, I don't own the home, but I am in charge of the home. What can I do for you?" she continued more politely.

"You see those children over there talking to some of your children?" I asked.

"Of course. They're carrying suitcases and bags. Surely you are not wanting to place all those children here with me? Arrangements have to be made..." I cut her off.

"No, no, not at all." And I began my story, "My point is that amongst my children are two very special little girls. D'avia is eleven years old. Mina is ten years old. D'avia's father shoved her down onto a track at a train depot in Stuttgart where other civilians crowded around and covered for the child, waving for her to go under the car. As a result of the chaos, her family was shot at that train depot in Stuttgart, Germany. Several people objected to the soldiers trying to separate their family to board the rail cars. D'avia is Jewish, you see. And, the other very special little girl, the little blond one, is Mina. She is the bravest soul I have ever known. She hid the Jewish girl in a bunker she built deep into the small forest next to the train depot. She hid this girl for two months with her self-created shelter almost completely underground. The little blond girl initially labored every day building a hole for what she thought would be a safe place for herself from her abusive mother. She must have dug for a month in February. She used her hands and a broken shovel. Surprisingly, she did amazingly well in her construction because she also provided a roof for the enclosure of what was available in this forest. Then one day she spotted the Jewish girl rolling under train cars and lying flat between rails under a couple of cars for long

157

periods of time. My little hero went and rescued the little Jewish girl and brought her to her bunker. She provided blankets and food for nearly a month before my children discovered her. We have been planning for weeks to escape and get my little Jewish girl and her rescuer to Switzerland to be safe. It was the closest country I could get to not involved in the war." I took a breath and continued, "Have I found a safe place for them or are you going to turn them away?" I boldly asked. The woman who starred directly into my eyes but hesitated.

After an interminable amount of time standing there looking at her, she said quietly, "You have found a safe place for them. They are most welcome here. I will make arrangements for a room for them. They will share with two other girls." The woman continued to look at me but with a softer gleam in her eyes. "Do they have any family that will be looking for them at some time later?"

"Sadly, no. The Nazi's executed D'avia's whole family in front of the crowd gathered. That would be her parents and two brothers," I kept a straight face, so I wouldn't start crying. However, tears welled up in my eyes despite my best efforts. "Mina's mother liked using her as a punching bag when her father smacked her mother."

There was a long pause for which I thought she did not understand me, then, "My name is Amelie Favre. What is yours?" she asked.

"I was using the name Eves Obermardt in Germany, so if you hear the children call me Eves they are trying to stay with the name and make no mistakes," I offered.

Amelie continued, "I do not need to know your real name. This is the Village of Children house. Many of the children here were placed by parents sending them away from the war with Germany. I have a few who were herded here in a group as orphans. There are parents, I believe, that will come looking for some of them. I do not know. If the parents are killed in the war, I may never know. But for now, they are my children. The house is big and run efficiently by me and a few staff and volunteers. However, volunteers show up every day to help with anything needed. The helpers are often from a Jewish community not far from here, but I also have some Jewish and Christian staff who work here for room and board. Are all these other children yours then?"

"For now, they are." Amelie gave me a curious side look and I knew she understood.

"Well, let me meet all the children anyway." She turned and walked toward the group of kids gathered. I sorted out mine. Then I began introducing Hans, Klaus, Lian, Ada and Clotilda. Lastly, I brought forward Mina. Her hair was stringy from not being washed and she seemed sullen, looking only at the ground. Next to her I introduced D'avia, her hair reflecting gold strands in the sun. She looked anxious but her gaze was directed at me. I squatted a bit and spoke to the two girls first and gently lay my hands on their shoulders.

"Mina, D'avia, this lady is going to let you stay here at the *Pestalozzi Children's Village*. You will be safe here. You are no longer safe in Germany. Do you understand?" I asked looking from one girl to another.

"You are going to abandon us?" asked D'avia.

"Is that what this trip was about, D'avia?" I asked.

"No, I know it wasn't. But I don't want you to leave." She began weeping. "I know you were rescuing us, but I love you. I will miss you so much." With this I felt lower than cow dung. I stood up and asked Amelie if there was a quieter place the kids and I could talk with the two girls. She said there was a picnic table behind the house. She would keep all the other children in their rooms for a little while. She began calling them and pointing to the various doors on all three levels below the artistic wood scroll work above the third floor. My children followed me around to the back of the house and we found the picnic table with which to sit at.

"Now, D'avia and Mina," I began, "you have been alone for so long in that bunker and look what you have here. A lovely new home, food you don't have to steal, beds to sleep in, and lots of kids to play with. Most of all, you're safe."

Mina stopped flinching. "No one here will ever hit you again. In fact, they will all protect you. Frau Favre will love you and care for you. You will come to love her too." I looked at both of them. I raised Mina's chin so I could see her eyes. She was weeping. I brought her and D'avia into a gentle but all-encompassing hug. They hung on me in response. I let the hug stay for at least a minute or more, my head between theirs. When I pulled away, I continued, "I will always love you both. You will always have a special place in my heart, and I will never, ever forget you. I need you to do this for me. I need you to be safe, so I can finish what I started. You understand?"

Both girls nodded sadly. "I have to get the others back to Germany. They have a job to do to fight the Nazis by helping other kids. Do you understand this?" They looked at each other and then back at me and nodded more definitively.

"Most important," I added, "you will still have each other. Neither of you will be alone. Is that some comfort to you? You will continue to be together and you will live together in the same bedroom," I smiled with this statement. Both girls looked at each other and smiled for the first time. They hugged. Therefore, we proceeded to say our good-byes. We needed to leave. Our time table was tight. Hans, Klaus, and Lian hugged the girls first without shyness or coyness, but openly and warmly. The girls were next. They did a group hug the four of them. Ada and Clotilda cried a little bit, but were alright for the most part. The two girls hugged the tightest to each other. I finally had to go and tap Ada on the shoulder. The kids and I moved back to the front of the house where Amelie was waiting for us sitting in an outdoor Adirondack chair. She rose and welcomed the two girls with open arms. They looked at each other again and then walked into her embrace. We left two suitcases and a bottle of milk for them and drifted down the drive. The original five children and I waved and waved in response to their waves and Amelie's. We waved until we were out of sight over the hill. We were all tired, but we needed to at least keep going to get back to Konstanz. This time we tried to hail a ride from anybody. Finally, a farmer came by with a horse-drawn wagon and told us to sit on top of the bags of grain. We were all on the verge of sleep, lulled by the wagon's motion.

Back in Konstanz, I had to send the boys to look for another boat. It was getting dark. I told them to pick a hiding place and watch until they had an opportunity without being spotted. The girls stayed with me near the shed we used previously. No one came to the shed, but we stayed behind it just in case. About an hour later, I woke Ada and Clotilda who had fallen asleep on the blankets we laid down. Lying beside them for that hour, we all kept fairly comfortable. I, of course, did not sleep. I listened for any sound that came near us. Mostly, I just heard the soft bustle of life here and there in the town. Commotion mostly came from merchants closing up for the night or well-wishers on the way home to their families. The boatyard made some noise as trawlers and an excursion boat came into shore. Returning the boats was almost concluded and it got quieter. I could hear men yelling at other men about boat stuff, but I was only focused on closer sounds. I thought I heard someone approaching the shed by the front, but I realized after a few seconds, he was just relieving himself in the brush nearby. He left.

Suddenly, the boys came around the east end of the shed and quietly signaled to me that it was time to go. I awakened the girls shooshing them as they woke up. We folded and rolled those most precious blankets and packed them into the rucksacks we carried. There was only the one suitcase left to carry, so I took it and Hans and Lian took two rucksacks while the girls and Klaus hoisted their rucksacks onto their backs. The hardest part was trying to sneak between hiding places to get across to the boatyard.

There was heavy cloud cover once again. We walked across the street, but most people paid us no mind. During our trailing among the boats, we had to cramp down or down right crawl in my case. The boy's thick stockings were wearing thin under their heavy coats. The girls also had thick stockings on but managed to kneel on the lower part of their dresses at times. Me, I had put the dress back on to come to town and cross the street, but once in the boatyard, I switched to pants. I never learned to maneuver in a dress under these circumstances.

We managed to cross the darkening Lake Constance quietly without event and docked the boat under an out-of-the-way barren tree and bush combination. When we climbed the banks to the German side of the town, it was too late for any trains that night, so we rested in the underside of a large row boat. With the blankets and body heat, we were warm enough to allow sleep for a couple of hours or so. I didn't know what time it was as I couldn't see my watch on my wrist. I just let my head loll back and closed my eyes. It seemed like minutes when I felt Lian shaking me. It was dawn and he felt we needed to plan.

First things first, the children drank some of the remaining milk and ate the sandwiches Amelie was kind enough to send off with us. I think I wolfed mine down, I was so hungry. Then, "People, what do you think we should do now? I think we can take the train at this point. Returning in the military staff car would be highly suspicious since I've been gone too early and too long. If there is increased bombing in Stuttgart, the SS or Gestapo, whatever, may be checking driver's papers as they enter the city. My papers and car won't work carrying the five of you, even in the trunk. I will have to change, of course, but there should be no problems with a mother and five children. I have the money. We have the passports and the papers will get us by if we don't bring attention to ourselves, or *I thought* if we bring too much attention to ourselves. We won't have anything to eat on the train, so I will see if I can buy any foodstuffs before we board. What are your thoughts?" I asked

"I am not entirely comfortable with riding the train," Hans said, "but only because I've never ridden one."

"Me neither," the rest of them chimed in.

"Alright, here it is. A train like this has compartments that people can sit in. We will get on the train after I purchase tickets and go to the nearest empty compartment. You will all sit like ladies and gentlemen, unless," I paused, they all leaned forward, "someone else wants to enter the car. Then you will get up and walk or lean on the seat making noise or stand at the window."

"In other words, we are to be obnoxious," Hans interpreted.

"Exactly. Although don't overdo it or we could get kicked off the train. Also, soldiers are more likely to just to pass our compartment not wanting to deal with antsy children."

Clotilda turned and asked, "They would kick us off in the middle of nowhere?"

"No, dobo, they would kick us off before we left the station if we were too annoying while people tried to board the car," Klaus answered.

"It's not necessary to be so rude, Klaus. She was just asking," Ada said.

"Klaus is always rude!" said Hans.

"Here, here, he is to me," Lian said.

I looked at them all standing in a rural area about five-hundred yards from the station. They were disheveled, tired looking, and a little irritable in their demeanor.

"Children," I started. They looked up at me. I had switched to my female attire and was very tired myself. I continued, "Stop acting like children!"

"Wha-a-a-t," said Lian wrinkling his nose.

All the children squinted at me in the bright sunshine.

"I said, 'Stop acting like children.'"

Klaus interjected, "What do you expect us to do?"

"I expect you to act like mature people who got me into this mess. I'm tired too!" I shouted.

The children began looking down at the ground and mumbling what sounded like apologies.

"Let's agree that we are all tired and that brings out the worst in all of us. Once we agree, then we can counter that with acting mature and behaving properly. You know how to fake it. Fake it," I said dryly.

"Ok, it's time to go to the station and look at the schedule, Eves," said Ada. The others nodded their heads and said no more But, before we moved, I told them to check each other out and straighten their clothes, brush them off, comb their hair, and stand up straight. It took about five minutes before we were ready to step out from the field. We made our casual walk on the road to the train depot dodging cars and loaded trucks on the nearby thoroughfare. There were shops opening or opened and I had the kids stroll with me while Hans went and checked out the train schedule. I was able to buy a loaf of bread and a few apples that were available. I also let Clotilda nab a hunk of cheese for us. Deeming our purchases enough for our trip, we joined Hans at the train depot.

Hans was waiting at the depot for us. He was excited when he saw the food we bought.

"Can I eat something now before we board," he asked, looking like a starving mountain lion.

I held him off with my hand, "What did I say about acting mature and like a gentleman?"

This was the first time I saw him act like a kid. His foot hit the platform in a stomp.

"Do I really have to act like your mother, Hans? Throwing a temper is going to get you absolutely nowhere with me," I said pointedly at him.

"It's just that I'm really hungry and I do all the running around to get boats and be a look-out and help hide everybody…" he said dwindling his speech.

"You are the oldest," I said.

"Being the oldest stinks," he replied head down.

"Yes, it does," I comforted him. "But, so does being the smallest like Klaus. Or being a girl in this era. Or being Jewish in Germany. Or challenging the German Gestapo. Or being afraid to read a book. Remember you came to me. I have had my difficulties, but I don't think I have let you down so far. And, I may yet lose my life before I can go back to my time. I'm risking quite a lot and you're complaining about being the oldest."

Hans gazed up at me with tears in his eyes. His tears began rolling down his face. "I never thought we'd make it, if you want the truth, and making it is harder than failing I realize now."

I pulled Hans to me and put my arms around him. He responded awkwardly but finally put his arms around me. I kissed the top of his head. "I know. I think we all know. But being the oldest is harder because you have more responsibility than the others. I've had to rely on you the most through all of this. You are a leader. Now you know what it is like being a leader. It gives you power but also great responsibility. You've done splendidly, my little man." With that I let him go and gently knocked foreheads with him as he gave me the tiniest little smile.

We finally boarded the train, found a cabin with no occupants, and proceeded to fill the overhead shelf with our satchels, and food on the seats beside our bodies. I needn't have worried about anyone wanting to come in. There wasn't much room for any other adult to be comfortable in my estimate.

# Chapter XXIV

Surprisingly, we didn't have much trouble finding a compartment. I acted naturally with five children and was almost inspected by a soldier who was checking passports. He looked at me through the glass unsuspiciously-probably he didn't want to enter a compartment with a mother and a large cadre of children. He passed us on quickly as I had prayed, he would. However, the train broke down and all passengers had to disembark and climb onto another train alongside that was commandeered to go to Stuttgart. This time there were occupants in every compartment we came to, so I instructed the children in a whisper to enter the first cabin occupied by only one person. I also told them to try and find one with a woman. They were able to comply in a matter of minutes. We entered a compartment occupied by a matronly woman of modest means, no fancy hat or expensive furs. She seemed more average of the public population in Germany with a plain little hat, and a scarf, what I used to call a *babushka,* and a well-worn dress. Her coat was lying beside her. It was wool of a brown color and heavy looking. She had low black heels with heavy stockings, not the streamlined nylon of the wealthy. Therefore, I gave the children the signal for sitting down and behaving. Only once did the woman speak when she looked from her newspaper and asked the kids if they wanted to sit by the window and lookout. She was more than happy to move toward the inside of the compartment. The kids agreed and agreed and arranged themselves by the window, sitting, some standing at the window. I politely thanked her and she just nodded her head. She did ask me where I was headed and I told her where as she commented she was going on to Berlin to see her nieces and nephews. I was a little surprised with the war well established. However, I did not know if Berlin was in any major trouble at this time. I just knew that there were more frequent bombings in Stuttgart but how effective the bombs were I had no idea. I made the requisite pleasantries with her, then rested my head against the wall. I fell asleep instantly. I saw or heard nothing.

Hours later, Hans woke me as we were coming into the station. I rubbed my face with my hands to become alert quickly. The view from the window was nothing like I had seen before. We were coming into a different part of the station that appeared to only have commuters of society. No Jewish platforms, no trucks dropping off victims, just an average train disembarking platform. When we descended the stairs, I saw the station was covered by periodic glass roofing. I thought we were in an entirely different station. Thus, I stopped a conductor unloading citizens and asked if this was, in fact, Stuttgart. He looked at me oddly and said, "Of course, madam." I was bewildered. Where were the outside platforms, the throng of hundreds of people with suitcases and children being herded onto rail cars. I must have look mystified because Ada asked what the problem was. I told her and she replied, "Eves, in case anyone overheard us, we are at the other end of the station.

"What do you mean 'the other end'?" I asked.

"Have you ever looked at the station from the front?" she asked.

"I guess not. We were always operating at the back near the forest."

"Of course. We need to take you around to the front of the building. Guys, do you want to go around the front, so Eves can see the whole station building?"

Hans replied, "That may not be a good idea. It's taking a risk that someone that knows her could be spotted. She has been gone from work for four days without contact with her boss."

Klaus added, "I'm not so sure. Her co-workers are all at her office. I'd like to show her how huge the front is."

Ada, Clotilda, and Lian all agreed.

"What could happen? There are so many people coming and going," Ada said.

"Alright," Hans added, "but we need to be careful all the same. Walking outright on the sidewalk may put us in some risk. Afterall, quite a few of the Gestapo and the SS are walking routes and arbitrarily checking documents."

"See, there is a new bomb shelter sign over there I never saw before," Klaus commented. Just then, a huge explosion shuddered the station. Everybody froze. "I guess their getting closer," uttered Lian. We waited to see if there was another explosion. There was, but it was further away to the northern part of the city. We looked at each other as if in a trance.

Finally, Clotilda wanted to be heard, "We can cross the main floor and go out the front, or one of the other doors behind the columns. Nobody is going to pay attention to a family."

"I'd rather go out one of the other doors behind the columns leading out onto the sidewalk. Then she can just look up from a parking spot in front," Hans replied, "Let's make it quick. Some people seem to be running."

We all had our luggage and walked at a mimicked pace of the other hurrying people crossing the main station. Within a few minutes, Hans directed us to one of the less obvious exit doors that emerged onto a walkway behind a row of columns. Once outside, the children guided me to an empty parking spot and I looked up.

"Oh, my God. I had no idea the station was so large. All I saw was a tall back building where the Jews were taken onto cars."

"That's because the Fuhrer Hitler did not want any of the Germany citizenry to see what they were doing to the Jews," answered Liam, "Most citizens did not know about the camps for a very long time. That's the way Hitler wanted it."

I was still in the middle of a fixed stare at the huge edifice of the main station entrance, when I heard my name called. I froze as the caller was behind me. I knew that voice and it terrified me. The children turned and saw a fair-haired man with a uniform including the peaked cap of a high ranking official. I refused to turn around, foolishly hoping the person would go away. I had no idea what to do. Finally, the person approached and tapped me on the shoulder. I slowly turned to see Herr Berchtold standing their angry and confused at the same time.

"You had better have a good explanation for yourself, Frau Obermardt. Where the devil have you been? No message, phone call; you just don't show up to the office for a week! And, why the suitcases!? I demand an answer." He exploded, then saw he was receiving attention yelling at a woman with children. He grabbed me by the arm and pushed me back behind the columns to the brick wall and down along the wall where there were no doors exiting and part of the wall was in deep shadow due to the time of day. His face came so close to mine I could smell alcohol on his breath.

"I want an explanation now!" he spit at me in hushed tone.

I decided I'd had it. The children were holding on to me and tugging to tell me to give him an excuse. I stepped closer and slid something from my coat pocket without him noticing. Neither did the children notice.

I, calmly and in a low tone, told him to his face, "I just rescued two young girls who were being abused and got them across the border to neutral country."

He looked completely confused now, "What! What does that mean and why didn't you just come to me? If they were being abused, I could have helped. And, why take them to another country?" It took him a few minutes staring at me before I saw the slow realization cross his face of what I had done. "They were Jewish," he whispered plaintively. "How could you? I'm the transport minister for Christ's sake. You betrayed me. You're a sympathizer," he said as a look of horror creeped over his face. He backed away only inches and just kept staring at me and then his eyes switched to the ground like he was processing the thought.

His stare returned to my face, "Do you have any idea what they will do to me if this is found out? My own assistant helps Jews escape transportation to the camps. I cannot let this become known." His eyes looked wild with fear enveloping his whole face. Quickly he pulled out his gun and pointed it at my chest. He grabbed my arm and moved me down the brick wall to an alcove recessed into the facade with a fixed bench against the wall. He came close to my face again and asked, "Are these children Jewish also? Are you Jewish?"

"No," I said quickly, "These children risked their lives to help me."

Berchtold gazed at them, children huddled together behind me, their rucksacks held up in front of them as protection. Berchold's eyes gazed at them, and his face cringed in anger or hatred. I couldn't tell which. Then he lost all expression, "Frau Obermardt, you are a traitor and an imbecile. I have no choice but to end this now." Berchtold withdrew his gun and slowly reached over and pressed his gun against the first rucksack, held by Hans behind me. I stepped in front of Hans in sync with his gun. A muffled but distinct sound erupted between us. Berchtold and I both spasmed. Suddenly the expression on both our faces changed to one of shock. Hans and the

171

others were frozen to their spots with their mouths aghast. Tears started rolling down their cheeks while Herr Berchtold and I held our stance for at least a minute. He instantly put my arms under his and held on. The shock of the action was almost too much to bear. We just looked at each other expressionless. We slowly turned our embrace toward the seats and gently sat down with each other. I could not stop staring into his eyes when they evolved from a bland look to one of confusion with his eyes glued to mine. I returned the look and held on to him. It was apparent that we were both in shock and trying to process what took place. The shot intended for Hans had gone into me. The handle of a knife was sticking out from just below his sternum.

Gradually, his face froze. I gently leaned him upright against the bend in the wall as I withdrew my trembling left arm from under his right arm, took his gun out of his right hand and returned the gun to his holster. I snapped the latch on it. I did all this with slow, methodical movements. The children slowly lowered their satchels and starred somewhere between Berchtold and myself. As I leaned back, they saw the knife sticking out of his chest angled upward surrounded by ragged edges of a red circle. The children suddenly scuttled forward to guard against any unwanted attention from in front of us. Once they turned sideways to look at the pair of us sitting, both sharing a small quantity of blood on our heavy coats, Clotilda seized with fear yelled in a whisper, "Who got stabbed!?"

"How-how-how did you do that?" asked Ada. They all noticed Berchtold slumping onto my shoulder.

I looked at her with fear in my eyes. "I have always carried a concealed knife with me for protection. I work or worked in the city of Chicago. I trust no one," I answered, "But, I have never killed anyone." I looked at Berchtold's face casually. "I could not let him hurt you children, even if I had to sacrifice my own life."

"But then your children would never have been born," said Clotilda in awe.

"I know. I had no choice in my view. There was no way I could let him harm you. He was going for you first, Hans, then the others to punish me before he killed me."

"Why are you crying?" asked Klaus.

"Have you ever killed anyone, Klaus?" I asked.

He concentrated his eyes on mine in a serious stare, "No."

"It is the worst experience to have. I didn't want to kill him. But, again, he gave me no choice," I said somberly. Then I bent forward with an "oofff" emitting from my mouth.

Hans put his hand on my shoulder, "You've been shot!!" The children went white-eyed with fear. "We have to move fast. We have to fix you up. Is it deep? Where did it hit?"

I replied, holding my side, "I pushed his gun away with my left arm. I think it is an angle shot."

"What does that mean?" Lian almost screamed?"

"It means that the bullet went under the skin but at a shallow angle out of the body, I think," said Klaus "Look for an exit hole in her back, Ada."

Ada responded instantly, "There is an exit hole not too far from the front hole!"

"You've got blood on your coat," Hans said then retrieved a blanket from one of the sacks, "Here, hold this." He handed me the blanket, a plaid patterned item. Hans laid it over my shoulder and across my chest like a swag. I stood up with some help from the girls. He removed a pin from the waist of his short pants and pinned it tightly just above my left hip. Then,

"Hold your hand with pressure against that side. We have to go now!" he strongly whispered.

As we began to move, I said, "Stop!" The children jerked in a collective halt. I returned to Berchtold's body and closed his eyes. Then, I looked around ahead of us but there were so many people focused on their own destinations that we were able to hurriedly slip down to the end of the brick station wall and around the huge end column. Hans grabbed my hand with his arm around my back. This hand joined Ada's hand at my back from the other side. Clotilda held Ada's hand and Klaus and Lian walked in front of me. We looked normal if that is even a word with a real definition.

"Where are we going, Hans?"

Suddenly, there was another booming explosion near us that threw us to the ground. Hans quickly threw himself over me as heavy debris rained down on us.

He screamed "We have no more time! Berchtold's death will be discovered any moment! We have to get you back!" He shouted at all of us. We realized the rucksacks were still on the bench back with Berchtold. I forgot that I had left him leaning on one with his right arm, head back as if he was napping.

"Forget it!" screamed Clotilda. Once up on our feet, we tried to match the pace of the bustling people around us in a hurry to get to safety. Hans was going to have us catch a tram that took us closer to the area where the *magic door*. That plan was abandoned when we saw the tram appeared damaged in the distance.

"We have to get her out of here!" shouted Klaus. So, the children veered me away from the direction of the house we had occupied and headed in the opposite direction to the park as quickly as I could move which wasn't saying fast. Eventually, in the park, I recognized the huge clump of bushes that hid the door. Fortunately, there were other clumps of large bushes all

174

over the park people were running by. We looked around and walked behind the bushes to avoid being seen. "Okay, Cully, we're on the wrong side. We have to sneak around inside the bushes. You might get scratched, so be careful. What he didn't know was that I was about to faint.

As Hans slowly led the procession, I did get stuck a few times. *Damn it!* I thought. Those bushes were as bad as holly bushes with their thorns. We finally edged to the side wall of the brownish-green door. We had enough room to huddle in the chilly air.

Hans piped up first, "You were magnificent, Cully." With that, he gave me a hug that I returned half-heartedly. He noticed. I began sliding down the wall.

"No, no, no!" said Ada. She and Hans got down beside me while the others stood by.

Hans motioned with his flapping hand to Ada who withdrew a small bottle from her jacket. Hans drew out a cloth, like a handkerchief, from his pocket, opened the bottle, and dabbed a little onto the cloth, then held it under my nose. I reacted instantly by shaking my head and becoming more alert.

"What was that," I asked.

"Vinegar," said Hans. "It would wake up anybody," Hans said gravely. "Can you get up?"

"I think so," I said as I felt revived.

Once I got up, the pain was there but Hans had stuffed some cloths inside my coat and repinned the sash.

"Hold your side. The bleeding has slowed. I packed it more. I really don't think the bullet hit any organs. The holes are too close.

Then Ada and Clotilda looked up at my face and said somberly, "We did it, Cully."

I hesitated to fully bring myself conscious. "Yes, we did," I weakly half-smiled, "But, I could never have done it without all of you, don't forget."

Klaus and Lian came up to me. Lian said, "I can finally say I am so happy."

Klaus added, "We were so right to come get you."

I asked, "You still haven't told me why it had to be me."

Ada answered, "Honestly, Cully, we only know that the two of them will be very important in the future. That's truly all we know."

"But, how do you know?" I asked again.

Hans looked at the others and bowed his head saying, "I'm sorry, Cully, we can't tell you. We would if we could, but we can't."

"Why can't you? There has to be a reason," I asked weakly frustrated.

"It would change what you know now, and we can't let that happen," Hans said a little sadly.

"Did you hear that?" shouted Lian in a whisper as he stooped. The others stooped with him and I bent over. "It's people coming."

"We have to get back," Hans said, "Cully, you go first. We'll be right behind you."

"You go first, children. I'll follow up the rear."

"Is your side going to hurt bending over?" asked Clotilda.

"I suppose so, but I want you all to be safe first," I answered.

"Your safety comes first! We'll be right behind you!" growled Lian.

"Okay, okay. I know you will turn back into elderly people, but will you be the same?" I asked.

Ada looked at me with compassion and tears brimming her eyes, "Cully, it doesn't matter how the outside package changes, we are still the same people inside."

"Alright, but may I hug you as children before we go back?" I said with raised brows.

The children looked at each other, but Klaus said, all moving toward me hurriedly, "Of course you can, gently. Cully, you were everything we could have hoped for in a savior."

I commented as we group hugged, and I lowered my head on top of theirs, "Well, actually, we were seven saviors, The six of us and Mina. It all started with Mina."

"That is true," said the withdrawing Hans nodding his head thoughtfully. "She is one brave soul."

I looked at each and every one of *my* children. As I backed toward the door holding my side, I took in the sight of them, and I stated, "I am proud to have been a part of this. It has changed my outlook on my life forever. Thank you for asking for my help." I turned and once again entered a curtain of electric buzzing. However, this time, the tingle in my feet and hands led to my mind and body tensing up. I saw flashes of light, and emerged within seconds. I felt different, in an exhausted state. I turned to see each child lined up behind me. Before I stepped to the door, I wanted to say something to each child.

"Hans, you will be a good leader in anything you pursue," I turned, "Lian, go to university any way you can. You have the makings of a brilliant scientist, doctor, or researcher," again I turned, "Klaus, you are strong in character. Your bravery will be important in your growing up," once again a turn, "Clotilda, you are going to make a difference in people's lives," turned for the last time, "Ada, you are wise, kind, and precious. You will be an amazing adult."

No one spoke, all smiled and each put a hand on me to turn me toward the door. They maneuvered me toward the door handle and I turned the knob which made a quiet squeaking sound. I looked back at the children behind me and said, "Stay close."

They all replied, "We will."

I opened the door slowly for just enough room for me to get through bent over. I held the door behind me for Hans. He grabbed the edge of the door and followed me in, or so I thought. The door closed with a soft thud as I was carefully descending the stairs hanging onto the wall. I thought there had been enough time for all of them to get through, but it was so quiet, thus, I turned my head.

# Chapter XXV

Cully was alone. She went back up the stairs and grabbed the doorknob, but it wouldn't open. She rattled it but it still wouldn't open, so she walked down the stairs to get help. Then she thought, *what help?* Pausing from weariness, she decided to put on her own clothing from the locker and place the other things neatly folded on the shelf. She unpinned the bloody sash, removed the coat, skirt, and blouse, dropping them in a heap on the bottom of the locker. Lastly, she removed her considerably bloody slip with the cloths. The hole in her side was bleeding again, so she tied her own shirt around her as tightly as she dared, while gritting her teeth, and donned her zip jacket. Cully slowly retrieved her 'real' purse. She removed nothing from the 'era purse' she had carried remembering she could take nothing with her from 1942. Thus, she wasn't sure, so she inserted the switchblade knife she used on Berchtold into the "era purse". Closing the locker, she then walked to the wardrobe to see if the waiter that came in before their *mission* could help her. She opened the doors cautiously. Cully looked in, surprised but not shocked. There hung many starched white shirts, shelves of string ties and white aprons. She knocked on the back of the wardrobe. It produced a sound of solidity. There was no false door. It just butted against the wall. *Ok*, she thought, *she'll run upstairs. Or, maybe, walk carefully.* Before she did, she carefully climbed up the stairs to the *magic door* and tried the knob once more. This time it gave and Cully pushed it open with anticipation. However, she was thrust into disappointment as she was exposed to a dark alley between two buildings. *This is very strange*, she contemplated. She closed the door and opened it again to the same scene.

Cully returned to the locker area and was prepared to climb up the few stairs to the restaurant. *I need to get help.* A couple of waiters brushed by her swiftly, tearing their long, white aprons off, ties, and shirts throwing them in a laundry bin in the corner of the room. They seemed startled at her presence and asked, "Oh, can we help you?"

She quickly answered, "I was looking for the bathroom."

"Oh, it's the other way," one waiter said sympathetically, pointing to the main dining room door. "You take a right from the dining room. People often get embarrassed trying to guess which way to go."

"Yeah, you'd think they'd actually put up a sign. So difficult," the other waiter cracked sarcastically.

The first waiter came back, "Oh, that would be tacky to put up any old sign," he seemed to be mimicking someone else. Looking at me, he added, "They're still trying to decide between three signs. Would you believe it? It's been five weeks. They want it to match the restaurant sign outside. Stupid," he shrugged.

"Thank you," and Cully left. She carefully climbed four stairs and looked to her right. What she saw, in her astounded pause, was behind a fancy divider. An elegant restaurant. It had white tablecloths, wine glasses at every table, candelabras at the side area, busy waiters in white shirts and black bow ties with white aprons wrapped around them. The many patrons were, of course, in contemporary clothing. She crept up another stair and a waitress came rushing around the corner in the same waiter's outfit, bumping her and saying, "Sorry, I'm in a rush." She took the stairs two at a time down. Cully looked back and knew the area she had visited was for the staff changing room.

When she ascended the last stair, she looked across at the familiar hallway to the bathroom door. Cully strolled across the alcove and turned left to enter the restroom. It was all aglitter with modern fixtures, a basket of hand towels, modern cubicles, and was immaculately clean. She faced the mirror. Cully spoke out loud looking into her own eyes, "It never dawned on me until I opened that door that the children were not coming back with me". She hung her head and turned in a daze heading for the dining room and realized she could not ask for help here. She made her way toward the entrance of the restaurant and opened the door. When it shut, she turned back. The door was red, but it had no porthole with bars-just a sign above it saying,

*"The German Restaurant Extraordinaire"*. It was still deep into the alley like before, but now it had velvet rope strung between brass posts all the way out to the street. She looked straight ahead at the waiting customers coming from the sidewalk. She had to excuse herself to move between them and the velvet rope to get away from the restaurant. Cully walked the six blocks to Union Station trying to process what happened in the last twenty minutes. She headed for her train home to Skokie.

Cully almost fell asleep on the train but forced herself to stay awake so she wouldn't miss her stop. She was exhausted. All that had happened from that morning till now was incredible to her. She almost felt like she dreamt it. But she knew it really happened. And then, she sat up hit with an anxiety. *What if what she did had a ripple effect? What if, because of her actions, something in history would go catastrophically wrong or bad?* Cully sat back and realized her world seemed the same right now, but she would have to read the papers, listen to the news, and do some research to see if her actions provided a course of manipulated events. She prayed all the way to her station that any affect would be positive and not malevolent.

Arriving at the station, Cully found her car. It was an odd feeling but she had to touch it to make sure it too was real, that it was her car. As silly as she felt, she was too tired to think. She simply unlocked it and drove to the nearest emergency center to get the hole in her side looked at. While driving, she did look around to see if anything looked different in her town, then in her neighborhood, but all was proving the same. She approached the ER and parked in the allotted slot. She strolled into the hospital holding her side and was attended to immediately. She was able to convince the treating physician she had fallen onto a metal rod that had come off her ironing board. Subsequently, the physician informed her not to remove things that stab you. She informed Cully that the injury will just bleed more. The doctor informed Cully that she had lost a good deal of blood and should stay overnight. Cully informed the doctor she wanted to be in her own house. Not unaccustomed to this reaction, the physician cleaned and mended both holes, gave her a script for antibiotics and a tetanus shot, and strict instructions to rest, drink lots of fluids, and to see her own physician for a follow-up in a couple of weeks.

Cully used the garage door opener and pulled her fourteen-year-old Lincoln sedan in next to her late husband's car-a BMW she called his '"beemer". She closed the garage, opened the connecting door, and proceeded to enter her quiet space. She cautiously stepped into the kitchen, then the living room. *Ahah! All was the same.* She felt assured and dropped her jacket and purse on the floor with her keys and headed for the front door. Quietly unlocking it and peering out, she saw a white tub overflowing with mail under her mailbox. *Oh, my God, I forgot to stop the mail!* She smacked her forehead with the heel of her hand. *What a stupid thing to think of.* Then she scrunched up her face. *I had no way of knowing how long I'd be gone. My life was so bizarre, how could I even think about stopping mail. Mail is so ordinary.* She cast her eyes down, stepped out onto the porch, picked up the basket, gazed around the dark street, and said out loud, "Thank God for ordinary." She abandoned the tub on her dining room table and climbed the stairs to the bedroom.

Once she put on her pajamas, she went downstairs to make some hot tea. She sauntered into the kitchen, turned the light on, and once again gazed around her perfectly clean, same, ordinary kitchen, and laughed. Checking the answering machine, she found several messages: some from work, two from her kids, and several from numbers she didn't recognize. She fixed her tea and decided *it will all be there tomorrow.*

Early the next morning, the phone rang and she flopped over on the bed smacking her hand on top of it. Her bleary eyes identified the answer button, so she pushed it.

"Hello," she said in a sonorous voice.

"Mom, where have you been? I've been calling you all week! I was getting scared. You're not supposed to be where I can't find you!" Mina said.

"I'm here, darling, just not awake."

"Mom, are you o.k.? Where were you?"

"What day is it? What's the date?" Cully asked.

"It's August 4th; it's Saturday. Why? Did you lose time or something?"

"You might say that. I was working so much overtime, I decided to go on a trip. I needed some *me* time after your father....sorry, darling, but you and David are always so busy, I didn't think to call and bother you," Cully said trying to stifle a yawn as well as calmly telling her twisted truth.

"Are you sure you're alright, about Dad? I don't want you to fall apart again or anything. I can fly home in a few days?" Mina suggested.

"Absolutely not. I am fine, baby girl. You go tackle your job. Anything else?"

"I got a promotion to Training Manager for the new hires on the lot. I'm management, Mom!" Mina practically shouted.

"Oh, honey, that's wonderful. Can I go back to sleep now? I've been up for fifteen hours and I'm not recovered to daytime person yet."

"Well, I suppose. I've got to get up in front of a hundred- and twenty-five-people Friday for my intro speech. I'm so nervous, my stomach is in knots," Mina said breathlessly. "Tonight, though we're going out to celebrate. I have been working on this promotion for months. I am so excited!"

"That's wonderful. How's your brother?" I asked.

"He's fine. I'm so glad he's out here with me. I have friends, but I like being able to see him more than when he lived in Skokie," she replied. "Also, he finally got the job with Paramount Studios. He's in marketing. He loves it. I know because he tells me like every time I see him," Mina jabbered at lightning speed.

"Did he try to call me too?"

"No, he's so busy, I don't think he's got time to sleep, let alone call you. That's why I'm calling for him."

"Sounds good," Cully really was drifting off again, "Call me after your party, so you can tell me all about it. And don't drink too much."

"MOM!"

"Okay, I know, I know. You're a responsible adult. I have to go, baby girl. I'm falling asleep again. Love you," she mumbled as she was hanging up. However, she did hear a whisper of "love you too".

Cully slept for a few more hours and, finally, got up to take a shower. She felt like she was washing months of sweat, grime, and dirt off of her body. It felt marvelous. Cully dressed, flew downstairs, got a cup of coffee and prepared to tackle the tub of mail. Yet, she paused. She retrieved the days newspaper and studied it for anything unusual. Nothing she could find.

Once again looking at the mail, she decided to leave it for the next day. *Sunday is a good day to do all that*, she thought.

She decided she needed some fresh air and the lake. Cully loved Lake Michigan, and all the museums and Buckingham Fountain by the lake. So, taking the train, she went into the city and did a nice, easy walking tour of her favorite lakeside haunts. She didn't want to stay too long, so she dropped by Marv's, her coffee shop. Marv's was doing a brisk business at Adams and Dearborn. She managed to enter this time without incident and headed for the queue. Marv had her coffee concoction memorized as he did so many others. Although, when she looked for a place to sit, that was difficult. Then, a stranger motioned to her. She walked over as he stretched his hand out indicating the seat opposite him. Cully thanked him, but was not indicating she wanted conversation.

Until, he said, "Well, at least I'm seated when you came in today."

Cully turned her head to look at him. Oh, my gosh. He was the man who shoved the door into my backside six months before. "It's you," she said surprised.

"Now, I'm embarrassed," he nodded his head down.

"Don't be. I can finally laugh, a little, now." Cully, unaware, had drained her coffee quickly.

The man looked over to her cup, "Please let me buy you another coffee. May I?"

"Yes, you may. That would be lovely."

The man jumped toward the counter and brought back two coffees like Cully's.

"Oh, you like the lattes too," she asked.

"Oh, yes, vanilla is my favorite go-to stimulator," he said.

Cully posed her chin on her palm and asked this man, "Would you like to talk?"

The man smiled at her and said, "I would." He continued, "I'm a widower three years now, one son still in college. I think he's becoming a professional student." And that began a conversation that lasted at least two hours.

Cully eventually told him that she had to catch her train home and asked if he took the train. Alas, he did not he told her. He had an apartment on the northside of the city. But he did ask if he could walk her to the station to which she agreed. When they got to the depot, they had exchanged phone numbers and addresses. They scheduled a night to have dinner to which she also agreed. He didn't touch her; just waved good-bye and said he'd see her Friday. Cully liked that he didn't try to touch her. To her, it showed respect for her comfort zone after such a sudden meeting. She had been lonely at times and would relish the date, but she knew in her heart that it would take a long time for her to get acquainted with someone she might think of romantically.

By the time she got home, she realized it was too late to go anywhere else, so she settled in with the news on her computer and heated up a frozen dinner package. As she was reading the *Insight* section, she saw an advertisement for the new section opening of the *Holocaust* Museum in Skokie. For some reason she didn't understand, her cheeks got hot and she clasped her hands on them, feeling ill and afraid. She also felt nauseous, dashed to the bathroom, and didn't quite make it to the toilet before she threw up. Getting a cold cloth, Cully sat on the bathroom floor and held the cloth over her face feeling better within a few minutes. She knew she had to go to the museum. The next day. But it wasn't open on Sunday. She would have to keep busy doing her mail and reading or watching T.V. all day to make the day pass quickly. She gazed at the mail on the dining room table and decided it could wait until the next day or two. She felt a residual tiredness that she felt would take a few days of rest to overcome. So, a good book was better, and a nice cup of tea at her bedside was more enticing.

Monday morning, Cully arose and meticulously dressed in a nice blouse and her good jeans. She was not going to work again. She would call in later. Her mission today was to go to the *Holocaust Museum* to see if anything stood out as unusual because of what she helped accomplish. She was determined to spend a few hours there if need be. Once she arrived at the museum on Woods Drive, she emerged from her car and gazed at the stately building. Her tear ducts swelled up, but she wiped them away as ridiculous. Her tour of the museum revealed nothing she hadn't seen before. The remodeling, except for the addition, which provided new rooms. The walls were paneled with rich wood and covered with the names of destroyed families. The somber lighting made the room seem like all who entered should be solemn and respectful. It was exquisite with brass plaques, a marbled wall, brass floor relief, and an eternal flame burning in the middle of a brass pit. Now Cully let her tearing drip down her face. She pushed on past the railroad car display, the glass cases of uniforms and prisoner clothing, the multitude of pictures that the Nazis took to carefully document all aspects of their kingdom and actions.

Cully found nothing out of place, nothing irregular in the information, no pictures that were inconsistent with the historical record. She decided to leave. She walked slowly around the building and saw a fountain outside in the distance. She decided to go look at it. As she left the building, she approached a plain concrete water moat with nine fountains in front of a plain concrete wall behind dotted with steel plaques. There was a large plaque at the endcap of the fountain which she read to herself:

# FOUNTAIN OF THE RIGHTEOUS

**THIS FOUNTAIN SERVES AS**

**AN ENDURING TRIBUTE TO**

**THE PRECIOUS FEW WHO RISKED THEIR LIVES**

**TO SAVE JEWS DURING THE HOLOCAUST.**

**KNOWN AS**

**"RIGHTEOUS AMONG THE NATIONS,"**

**THESE VALIANT RESCUERS ARE**

**REMEMBERED HERE FOR THEIR**

**EXTRAORDINARY COURAGE.**

The plaque was donated as were most of the items in the museum. There were plaques of steel with rivets posted every couple of feet or so with names of individuals that had helped protect Jews during WWII. Cully imagined either to escape, hide them, or employ them as a necessary workforce. She strolled from the left passed the center and toward the right of the fountain reading names and what countries in which they operated. She was fully weeping thinking of the two little girls she helped escape abuse and the Nazi's death camps. She read each and every name. She was sad, but proud of each person on each plaque. When she finished. She sat on a bench behind the fountain to rest and reflect. Cully brought out a tissue to wipe her face and clean up her running mascara. Then she sat up straight to stretch her back and in front of her were more plaques. Most notably was one on the left where she sat. She became stunned to her very core, the breath held in her lungs. The plaque in front of her read:

### KLAUS GERHART

### BELGIUM

Two plaques down read:

### CLOTILDA KAPPEL

### FRANCE

The very next one read:

### HANS OBERMARDT

### POLAND

Three more down read:

### ADA FRIETAG OBERMARDT

### POLAND

The next one read:

### LIAN KURT

### GERMANY

The next one read:

### MINA BECK KURT

### GERMANY

Cully slipped down onto the grass and broke into huge, wracking sobs. She wasn't sad. She was so proud of all of them. She cried so hard; her chest pained her. The fact that they came to her for help was unimaginable to her now. These kids whose lives were inscribed in steel for all to see had needed her. She thought she would never understand why. However, a new feeling came over her. Pride. She was so honored to have been a part of one of their missions that she was beside herself, initially with grief that morphed into shock, incredulity, and, most of all, love for the children with which she spent such precious time. She finally lay down on the grass and cried herself to sleep. No one bothered her. It wasn't that unusual to see someone crying at this building site.

Cully managed to get home with tears still running down her face. She went directly to her computer to see what she could find out about Klaus Gerhardt. She went to the Holocaust website and entered his name into the search bar. There he was. His picture as an adult. The article summarized that *Klaus Gerhardt contributed to the rebellion against the Nazi Regime by becoming a member of the Edelweiss Youth Rebels as a child of 15. His earliest act of courage demonstrated his commitment when he single-handedly took out the tower at the Stuttgart train depot, which supervised the transfer of Jews to a number of concentration camps such as Dachau, Schirmeck-Vorbruck, Natzweiler-Struthof, and Fuenfbrunoren. This action culminated in complete chaos as the tower that controlled train car arrival and loading fell in the explosion with heavy damage to the south wing of the train station. Fortunately, the damage remained irreparable due to improved bombing techniques used by the Allies to destroy Stuttgart's essential and multiple industries as well as much of the city itself. Gerhardt continued in the underground rebellion evading capture throughout the war. Gerhardt lived to the age of 88 years succumbing to pneumonia and passing surrounded by his wife, Ada, also a member of Edelweiss and then the underground, two children and other family.*

Cully sat back on her chair and stared at the article. She had known this amazing person. She didn't know whether to cry again or just sit. Intense crying occurred during grief or prideful love. *She basically could cry forever* she thought. She slowed her breathing and decided she had to force herself to get back to her current reality. She needed to get back to her world and the people in it for which she cared. She would never be able to tell anyone about her adventure. But she promised herself to think of them now and then and keep her memories of them alive in her mind. Cully put her computer to sleep and went back to the dining room where the bucket of mail awaited her. This time she went to the kitchen and pulled out a bottle of scotch whiskey. Opening her precious bottle of Glenlivet, she poured a generous amount over a couple of ice cubes in her nice 'bar-type' glass. Strolling into the dining room once more, she found a coaster and placed it beside one of the center chairs. Cully decided to first separate the mail between obvious advertisements and envelopes. It took her no more than twenty minutes to accomplish this with a little help from the effects of the smooth scotch. Once that was done, she decided to toss all advertisements into the 30-gallon garbage can she brought in from the outside. Next order of business was the pile of envelopes. She leisurely picked up each item deciding whether it was another advertisement or an actual piece of significant mail. To the best of her ability, she sorted through them occasionally being forced to open one here or there that looked authentically important only to find out it was another advertisement. Her pile of junk mail piled higher than the significant pile until she finally finished with the last piece. She hadn't really registered who the envelopes were from, just what they looked like from the outside. She shoved more junk mail into the garbage can next to her seat and decided to open the "real" mail.

There was a bill, and another bill, and information on changes in her credit card account, and two notices from the city about work that was going to be done on her street in the coming weeks. She did most of her billing on line, but hadn't updated a few accounts. She received a letter from the funeral home that buried her husband wishing her a happy birthday. *That*, she thought, *was just creepy.* She tossed it immediately into the bin. She had forgotten about her birthday. Thus, there were more birthday wishes from clothing companies she patronized, the car dealership, and so on. She didn't feel much like celebrating, but it was in a couple weeks, so she'd think about it later. She savored the warmth enveloping her from her scotch. She kept going. As she sorted through what looked important or could wait, she noticed a stiff FedEx envelope from her mother's lawyer. She couldn't imagine who would be sending her such a missive. She stripped it open and into her lap fell a stiff Global Express envelope. She picked it up scratching her brow wondering who wrote in such elegant script on the envelope. The address was to her mother's lawyer's address downtown; the return address was strange being from Europe until she saw the bottom line of the city and country. It was from Konstanz, Germany. What?! It can't be. One of the eight children found her and wrote to her? *Weren't they all deceased?* She asked herself. She was holding her chest and began to hyperventilate. Then she slowed her breathing and very carefully looked at the return address again. There was no name on the return address. Thus, she turned the envelope over and pulled the zip string opener and out slid a regular envelope with the same address and return. She used her letter opener to slide very slowly across the top flap as if she was afraid, it contained anthrax. Carefully retrieving what appeared to be four or five hand-written pages, she put the envelope down with the opener, smoothed open the sheaf of pages, and began reading slowly, her eyes looking down at a steep angle. She was actually a little afraid. The date was the same as the day she returned from her *mission!* Then it began:

*Dearest Cully,*

*I have been searching for you for a long time. Let me begin by telling you that I knew your mother, Adele. She left Germany in 1961 at the age of fifteen. She had been out at night and actually spotted the Communist thugs building the wall between East and West Berlin. She decided to pack her belongings and run past the wall before it was completed. She pleaded with me to take what I could and get passed the wall before it was closed. We did as she said, however, before we got close with our running, I fell and injured my knee badly. I screamed for her to go through. She didn't want to, but I kept screaming at her till she left me. She arrived on the west side of Berlin as they were closing in on the last few yards of open space. By the next morning, the wall was completed. Surprised reactions and riots on both sides of this new wall produced chaos the next day. However, the riots in East Berlin were put down quickly. The soldiers at the border shot innocent people who tried to rush the wall. I could not believe my eyes. I knew of the political turmoil but never imagined something as that would take place.*

*Only Adele had visited the west side of Berlin often. I worked in the eastern part of the city and stayed close to home busy with the shops and caring for the house. I visited a few times to see a dear friend and then, just like that, we were cut off. I tried to get a hold of my friend, but all communication and visiting was forbidden. It was like being in prison, but outside. I thought of the Jew ghettos during the war. I was trapped. I made the best of it.*

*When Adele arrived on the west side of Berlin, there were very kind people to help her. The confusion and noise in the streets that first day, August 13 was miserable. I tried to inquire of my friends on the west side and was summarily turned away by the new government office. I talked to other people, but it was like that side of the city just disappeared. I was so very sad. I grieved all that year. Adele wrote to me upon arriving in the United States. The letter had been opened. It was obvious. She met a young man there and soon married. She lied about her age and said she was seventeen. She was a very mature beautiful girl. Adele wrote only occasionally since sending the letters to Germany was expensive. Plus, they took a very long time to get to me. When one letter did get through, she explained that she grieved because she was ashamed to have been one of the people to make it out. Thus, she denounced religion and her German citizenship. She was an American citizen as were her children. She said she was very sorry when I reported that letters she sent with money, did not always reach me. She said she loved me, and what happened in Berlin terrified her. She was now miles away from it. She began a new life. She wished me well often with sadness in her heart.*

*I wasn't going to give up. I was able to find her last address, by searching with the help of a professor at university here in Berlin after the wall came down in 1989. I moved to the west side of the city and began going to night school for nursing. It took a long time to locate Adele's address even with his help. By the time I found her address, it was too late. I discovered she had been killed in an accident riding a horse. I was devastated. I found out she was a widow at the time. I felt so discouraged. However, I tried again to contact any people who handled her possessions and was able to locate a lawyer handling her affairs. Agencies in the former West Berlin were miraculously helpful compared to the East. The lawyer, Mr. Gleason, was so helpful and gave me much information about her children. He gave me his address to make sure the package would reach him. Although, he instructed me to address the inside letter to you. He would then forward it to you.*

*I hope this letter will find you. I must tell you that I very much would like to get in touch with you. You see, Cully, Adele was my daughter. She used her married name only which was Sherman. However, her maiden name, my darling, was Schellenburg. She was Jewish by birth. I planned to marry her father. He saw an opportunity to escape through a tunnel to the*

West. He returned for me. I am sorry to say my beloved David was shot before he could get to me.

I am your grandmother, Cully. I left West Berlin and moved to Konstanz, Germany from which I have a fond memory. I would love to tell you about it. I have a small, lovely cottage. I hope you will want to visit with me by phone. (+49 37 9018207) I would love to talk to you and find out about my daughter's life ...and that of her children. I can only pray that you are as interested to contact me. Mr. Gleason assured me you would be.

With all my love because you exist,

D'avia Schellenburg